PRAISE FOR
THE BUS RIDE

The frenzied rush to see a friend or loved one before his or her passing is a trek that many if not most of us have had to make. Part fiction, part family memoir, Richard D. Bank's *The Bus Ride* takes us on such a journey. We travel coast to coast, from Depression-era Los Angeles to Philadelphia, environments etched with vibrant precision through Bank's tireless research and incandescent prose. We follow teenage Lou as he encounters, among many, Sister Aimee McPherson, a divorcee in Reno, the Japanese actor who played the first Charlie Chan. We pass through the forbidding cultural terrains of rising Nazism, a KKK rally, anti-Asian prejudice, a "Colored" waiting room in St. Louis, a Hooverville of 5,000. Warmly observed, this touching book is more than a bus ride. It is a journey of the spirit. It is a journey into the America of the 1930's. It is a journey into the heart of a Jewish family whose alliances and tensions might be those of any family. It is a ride you will be glad you have made.

— Harry Ringel, author of *Shemhazai's Game*
and *The Phantom of Skid Row*

MORE PRAISE FOR
THE BUS RIDE

Richard Bank's tenth book involves a cross-country bus ride and filial love of a son and his father. Tender, witty, avuncular, even humorous at times, Bank is at his best in this historical narrative of an early 20th century migration of his family from their Fairmount section of Philadelphia residence to Los Angeles and back with a cornucopia of events that happen in between that are both entertaining and tragic, but always told in a deft narrative style. Like other Bank novels, there is the quintessential Jewish setting for his characters, but in *The Bus Ride*, that cultural backdrop is superseded by themes that are pan-ethnic and universal, themes of life and loss, hope and fear, love and sorrow, encapsulated in a narrative of unbounded love of a son for his father.

— Patrick Vitullo, author of *The Lighthouse*

A deeply moving story of one family's commitment to their heritage, faith and traditions while striving to live the American Dream against the harsh realities of the Great Depression. Follow young Lou Bank on a cross-country bus ride that tests his—and our own—ties that bind. A worthy read!

— Harriet G. Fry, author of *Rum Raisin Rendezvous*

The Bus Ride

Richard D. Bank

www.auctuspublishers.com

Copyright© 2023 Richard D. Bank

Book and Cover Design by Colleen J. Cummings

Published by Auctus Publishers
606 Merion Avenue, First Floor
Havertown, PA 19083
Printed in the United States of America

All rights reserved. Scanning, uploading, and distribution of this book via the internet or via any other means without permission in writing from its publisher, Auctus Publishers, is illegal and punishable by law. Please purchase only the authorized electronic edition.

ISBN 978-1-7334456-2-7 (Print)

ISBN 978-1-7368278-3-3 (Electronic)

Library of Congress Control Number: 2023932938

Dedication

In Memory of Dave and Celia Bank
In Memory of Herman Bank
For my Dad

Authors Note

In the numerous workshops and classes where I have taught creative nonfiction, also known as narrative nonfiction, I informed my students that the generally accepted definition of the genre is "a work of nonfiction that utilizes the literary techniques of fiction." While allowing and even encouraging artistic freedom and individual style, I tolerated little deviation from adherence to facts and the truth other than insignificant details covered under the umbrella of literary license. Despite numerous lapses and even some total fabrications in the publishing world, as well as an effort to re-name the genre—the "nonfiction novel," I still adhere to my earlier sentiments. Therefore, much as I would like to, I cannot call The Bus Ride a work of creative nonfiction.

That said, my primary motivation in writing this book is to share my father's story about his coast-to-coast bus trip, traveling alone at the age of sixteen in June of 1933, after being informed that his own father was on his deathbed at the other side of the country, as well as depicting the events leading up to and following that journey. In a way, this tome is his memoir, and in fact, I possess a half dozen pages written in my dad's own words about this time in his life and I recall some of the things he said about it. But this book is also a story of a family, a people, a milieu, and a place and time in the history of our nation. Most of the characters did indeed exist; the places are real; encounters and conversations did occur; episodes were lived; relationships, confrontations, emotional struggles are revealed. Nonetheless, to make for an even more compelling and fulfilling narrative, I have taken the unbridled liberty to make stuff up and to fill in the story where facts were unobtainable.

Thus, I call this book a novel. I hope you enjoy the ride.

PART ONE

Cecelia (Mimitzerl) and David Bank

Boyle Heights, Los Angeles
June 1931-June 1933

Chapter One
Breed Street Synagogue

In the summer of 1931, Dave Bank, along with his wife, Celia, and their two sons, Herman, age 16, and Lou, age 14, arrived in the city of Los Angeles not because they necessarily wanted to but because they had to. Worn and weary from the 3,000-mile train trip, with Celia leading the way, the family weaved through the crowded station platform, down a flight of steps, and entered an elegant waiting room. The foursome gawked at the marble wainscoting and fine woodwork of the massive chamber as they ambled to the front doors leading out of the stately white stucco edifice and exited the building. Though still early morning, the sun's rays burst onto their faces, forcing the four pairs of eyes to narrow. The warm air was not unlike that left behind in Philadelphia, but the fact it would dominate the weather for a much longer portion of the year is what prompted them to undertake this journey in the first place.

Staring at the sun, Lou sneezed.

"Gesundheit," Celia said, plunking her bags on the pavement and the others promptly doing likewise. Celia

took a deep breath and took in her new surroundings, her blue eyes still squinting from the bright sunshine. Soon everyone was scanning the street bustling with cars and trollies and people crossing haphazardly.

"Over there, Mom," Herman said.

"Where, Chaim? Where?"

Herman pointed to a row of taxis along the sidewalk. Lifting their luggage, the group made a beeline to the first available cab. The cabbie drowsily pulled himself out of the vehicle, opened the trunk, and returned to his seat behind the wheel. After wedging in their baggage, Celia and the boys piled into the backseat while Dave slid in front next to the flabby-faced cabbie.

"Where to?"

"Breed Street Synagogue," Dave answered.

"Where?" The driver sneered.

Dave slipped his hand into his trouser pocket, withdrew a slip of paper, and replied, "Two-four-seven North Breed Street in Boyle Heights."

In 1858, a rugged Irishman named Andrew Boyle plopped down $4,000 he had earned for fighting in the Mexican-American War and purchased twenty-two acres on the bluffs overlooking the Los Angeles River where he intended to build his home. At the time, he surely would have found it incomprehensible that seven decades later the barren landscape would transmogrify into an area of six square miles comprising the ninth ward of the city of Los Angeles with a population exceeding 100,000 residents. What would have likely elicited an even greater rise from the Irishman's bushy eyebrows was that over seventy percent of the populace would consist of Mexicans, Japanese, Yugoslavs, Armenians, Russians, and Jewish immigrants from Eastern Europe. One can only imagine how Andrew and his son-in-law, William Workman, an early mayor and city councilman, would have felt making their way through the teeming Jewish neighborhoods that taken together held the distinction of having the highest Jewish population in the western half of the United States. Which, for Dave and Celia Bank and their two sons, made Boyle Heights a suitable place to live as well as the fact it was a mirror image of the Jewish neighborhood they left behind in Philadelphia. Even more, it was home to a large contingent of the Bank clan, formerly known as Michelbank, most of whom were congregants of the Breed Street Synagogue.

As the taxi approached its destination, the occupants peered at the brick structure, looming in the distance, that was constructed a decade earlier to replace the original wooden building that had served as a *shul* and religious school. Despite its massive size, there were still times when the new building struggled to accommodate the largest orthodox congregation west of Chicago. The synagogue's exterior was imposing with its unreinforced masonry, veneer brick, and cast stone embellishments on the façade. Dave was particularly taken with the brickwork and foliage carvings, while Celia could feel her chest swell with pride when she spotted the Star of David in bas-relief cast stone.

"Are you sure this is the right synagogue?" Celia asked Dave, her eyes still fixed on the Star of David. "It's so big... I've never seen such a *shul*..."

The Bus Ride

"This is what my brother, Max said," Dave answered matter-of-factly, reaching into his pocket to settle with the cabbie as the taxi pulled up to the curb.

"And Mordche and Avram will also be here?" Celia asked.

"Yes, yes, your brothers Max and Abe will be here too," Dave replied, referring to his brothers-in-law by their English names. "Now let's go."

"What about Uncle Sam from Vineland? Is he here?" Lou asked about his father's other brother who, along with Uncle Max, had been Dave's partner in a tailor business in New Jersey and were the only two of the four uncles who had migrated to California that Lou remembered having ever known.

"Both Uncle Maxes will be here and Uncle Abe as well. Just not Uncle Sam. Now let's go," Dave said, heading to the rear of the taxi.

Celia and the boys piled out from the back and retrieved the luggage Dave was removing from the trunk. Tugging at his jowls and sticking his head out the window, the cabbie harrumphed his impatience, and the instant the trunk snapped shut he put pedal to the metal, leaving the quartet standing alone on the deserted sidewalk with their suitcases, bags, and boxes beside them.

Looking as lost and forlorn as they had when they disembarked the ships bringing them to America two decades earlier, Dave and Celia, along with their two sons, appeared like a cluster of trees in the center of a desolate plain—trunks with few limbs and the tips of barren branches brushing against one another. Dave was of average height, standing a couple of inches taller than his wife and eye to eye with his sons.

"Why won't Uncle Sam be here, Pop?" Lou asked.

"He can't. He lives in San Diego. But we'll see him soon."

"Even if he lived next to the synagogue, he wouldn't be here! Not for a million dollars would your brother step foot inside a *shul*," Celia said, smirking at her husband.

"What do you mean, Mom?" asked Lou.

"Just that he and your father—"

"What, Ceila? What? Say it! The boys know I don't go to *shul*. To go once a week and pray for forgiveness for the terrible things you have done and promise to be a better person? And then once out the door, go about your business the same old way, not caring about the people you work with, or who work for you, or the way the bosses treat the work… workers.…" Dave bent over coughing, forcing him to stop and take deep breaths while Celia held his shoulders and the boys looked on anxiously. After a moment, the spasms ceased, and he lifted his head and straightened his back. "Enough of this. Services must be almost over," Dave said, glancing at his wristwatch. "Let's get closer to the door."

The family gathered their belongings, shuffled along, and repositioned themselves near the flight of steps leading to the synagogue's entrance.

"How do you know they'll be here, Pop?" Herman asked.

"Because Max checked the train schedule and said we should be getting in on Saturday morning, which we did, and they will be here until one, when services end," Dave answered, looking at his wristwatch again. "And's it's almost that now."

"What about Aunt Supa? Will she be here?" Lou asked.

The Bus Ride

"Maybe," Celia answered. "And perhaps your aunts Beilah and Ida."

"That's if they don't mind sitting behind a wall or up in the bleachers," Dave snickered, referring to the Orthodox practice of separating the women and men during services. Celia glared at her husband. Receiving the silent message, Dave said nothing further on the subject.

"Wasn't your brother's first wife Beilah's sister?" Herman asked his mother.

"Yes, she was, Chaim," Dave offered. "Beilah married Max after her sister, Sura, died when they were still in Russia. It was not unusual for a widower or a widow to marry the sister or brother of their deceased spouse. Sometimes, it was even considered a responsibility."

"Pop, tell me again why both Uncle Maxes have the same last name?" Herman asked, shooting Lou a mischievous look with a twinkle in his eyes.

"They're sort of... cousins...." Dave squirmed. A slight smile spread across Celia's face as she took a touch of perverse pleasure at her husband's growing discomfort. Lou had to avert his eyes while he bit the insides of his cheeks to keep from giggling.

"And Mom's name had been Michelbank like yours. Right, Pop?" Herman added with an ingenuous gaze. Celia's smile vanished, and her husband's face stiffened.

"Yes. You already know that." Dave's shoulders squared, adding some height to his slender frame, something he had always been prone to do when feeling defensive but even more so in recent years given the frailty of his health. "Your grandfathers—my father, Chaim, for whom you are named, and your mother's father, Elconin, were brothers."

Though Herman and Lou knew that while not the norm, it was not uncommon nor illegal where their parents came from for cousins to marry. However, in their new country, it was considered inappropriate and sometimes even unlawful for first cousins to do so. Which was why their marriage certificate listed Cohen, a common Jewish name and the one which Celia substituted as her surname instead of Bank, the name assigned to her, and most of the Michelbanks, when she arrived in 1908 at Ellis Island. Once Herman was able to contain his chuckling, he proceeded to take advantage of one of the few times he had the upper hand over his parents.

"You know, Pop, with two uncles named Max Bank and so many aunts and uncles and cousins on both sides of the family having the same last name, it really gets confusing—"

"Enough!" Celia shouted at her sons whose flushed faces attested they knew they had gone too far. "You both know very well that my father, Elconin, was your father's uncle, and your father's father, Chaim, was my uncle. All of their children—me, your father, the Maxes, Abe... all the others—are cousins! Now enough!"

Abruptly, as if a dam had burst, the synagogue's two massive front doors swung open, causing a swell of people to pour down the steps and flood the sidewalk. Sabbath services were a solemn occasion, and the men were appropriately accoutered in gray, brown, or dark blue suits with more than a few wearing yarmulkes and most others donning fedora hats. All wore ties over plain or striped cotton shirts with attached collars. Likewise, the women wore their finest dresses with wide shoulders, puffy sleeves, modest necklines, and mid-calf flared hemlines. Though head coverings were not required of females, almost all the ladies wore close-fitting hats with brims, sometimes ensconcing one eye. With practically everyone uniformly attired, Celia and Dave found it difficult to detect their siblings amidst the rising tide of bodies flowing over the walkway and into the street. Out of the surge arose a shout familiar to Celia.

"Mimitziral! Mimitziral!"

Celia's boys saw their mother swivel her head in the direction of the outcry, and seconds later her face radiated and her blue eyes sparkled while she wildly waved both arms in delight. Sprightly stepping into the crowd, Celia's feet were suddenly swept out from under her by a pair of outstretched arms wrapping themselves around her torso and lifting her off the ground, a feat impressing Lou and Herman because the man was barely an inch or two taller than their five-foot four mother. The man mirrored their mother's smile, and his matching azure eyes left little doubt that this was one of her brothers.

"Mordche! Oh, Mordche," Celia cried hugging her brother Max.

"Mimitziral!" Another man shrieked, running up and throwing himself upon his brother and sister. "You're here! You're here, Mimitziral!"

"Pop. What's with the Mimitziral?" Herman asked his grinning father watching his wife reunite with her brothers after a decade apart.

"It means little Celia," Dave replied, his eyes glued to the joyous scene. Herman and Lou studied the two men. "But Pop, they're hardly any bigger than Mom," said Lou. Dave laughed. "It's not about height, Lou. It's because your mother's the youngest. Max is seventeen years older and Abe nine years older, and your Uncle Ben in Philly is eleven years older. Mom was always the little one." Dave smiled again, spotting the tears running down his wife's round cheeks.

Celia's husband and sons continued to observe the siblings. Both men did indeed look much older to Lou than his thirty-five-year-old mother. The one Celia called Mordche was clearly the eldest, Lou concluded, after studying his deep-set eyes surrounded by wrinkles and the fedora hat that had slipped back, revealing a receding hairline. Gazing at his Uncle Abe, Lou saw the same full lips, inviting eyes, and softness of skin that he and his sister shared.

Suddenly, two women joined the group. Though not with the same enthusiasm as the men, they reached out their arms and injected themselves into the intertwined bodies exuding hugs and kisses and cries of joy in Yiddish, making it mostly indecipherable to Herman and Lou. Lou's eyes fixed upon the older of the women, who evinced the sweetest smile he had ever seen, while the other woman's lips were tightly drawn, permitting just a smidgen of a grin. The fervor of the reunited siblings was causing such a commotion that people nearby slowed their leave-taking to gaze upon the spectacle, causing Lou to blush and step away. His retreat from the scene

The Bus Ride

was halted in its tracks when his mother looked his way and fixed her stare directly upon him. Lou froze where he stood while Celia and the others floated like an amoeba over the sidewalk, not halting until they reached Dave and the boys.

"Lou, Herman, this is your Uncle Max and your Aunt Beilah," Ceila said, pointing to the older brother and the woman with the beaming smile. "And this is your Uncle Abe and Aunt Ida," she added with Lou becoming leery of Ida's formidable, fixed frown. "You remember them, don't you?"

Both boys nodded though Lou had no recollection of any of these uncles and aunts. He watched his father shake hands and hug the men warmly since they were not merely brothers-in-law but also cousins. There was a little more formality as he kissed each of the women on the cheek, with Beilah smiling broadly and Ida, whom Dave called Chaika, grudgingly allowing her frown to form a simper.

"Dave! Dave!" A man and woman were shouting as they barged through the mass of congregants and worked their way to the burgeoning Bank clan.

"Uncle Max!" Lou and Herman shouted simultaneously, easily recognizing their father's brother, who, until just a few years earlier, had also lived in Vineland, New Jersey where, along with Sam, the three brothers operated Bank Brothers Clothing Factory.

The boys also knew Supa, Max's wife, and their son and daughter who were the same ages as Lou and Herman. Like their father, Max had a full head of hair which was worn short and parted to the side, a no-nonsense face, and was below-average height. Looking at his father and three uncles, Lou could not figure out where he came from, since he was already as tall as them, and people kept telling him he'd be a six-footer one day.

Max fell upon Dave, and the two brothers vigorously shook hands and embraced. Dave politely kissed Supa on the cheek, avoiding the glasses precariously balanced on the bridge of her beaklike nose. Totally absorbed with the reunion and everyone talking and gesticulating at the same time, the siblings and cousins blindly coasted through the crowd which parted as the Red Sea had for the Israelites while Lou and Herman brought up the rear, slogging along with the suitcases, bags, and boxes. After a couple of blocks, the sidewalks were nearly deserted with most stores closed for the Sabbath and the congregants having peeled off in all directions, either walking to their homes, observing the ban on travel during the holy day, or to their cars parked far enough from the *shul* to avoid the wrath of the rabbi or one of the more zealous worshippers. Abruptly, everyone stopped.

"Well, what do you think?" Uncle Max asked his sister while beaming and pointing to a shiny black car parked along the curb. Lou and Herman gaped at the vehicle though neither could identify the make. "It's a brand-new Chevy sedan with six cylinders! The best money can buy. Not a Model A like that anti-Semite Ford puts out!"

"It's beautiful, Mordche," Celia answered. "I'm glad you are doing well."

"Indeed, Mimitziral, I am. Thanks be to God," her brother added, glancing at his wife, Beilah, who smiled

The Bus Ride

her broad smile and lifted her eyes unto heaven. It also didn't hurt, Dave thought, that Max had done very well for himself in Russia before coming to America in 1914 already a prosperous man.

"And for you and your family, my Mimitziral, I have a nice unit in an apartment building I own where you can live for practically no rent—just enough to cover utilities and taxes and such." Max pronounced. "You can even shop at Beilah's grocery store—it's on the first floor!" Max beamed again, and Beilah smiled. Lou observed his aunt's grin continue to expand until it consumed her entire face, and he wondered to himself if she ever spoke or only smiled.

"Max, you needn't have done this.... We can find our own...."

"Nonsense!" Max cut Dave off. "What else is family for if not to help?"

Everyone vigorously concurred, nodding their heads and crooning words of accord. Family was the keystone of the Bank clan and probably the only thing they could all agree upon, which, given its size, was a major accomplishment. Most of the family now resided in California with the recent addition of Dave's brother Louis, who, along with his wife and children, also lived in Los Angeles while Dave's sister Celia remained in Philadelphia with her family. Though rarely spoken of, there had been another sister named Fannie who died in Russia under mysterious circumstances when a teenager.

"Ok! Let's go!" Max thundered. "Everyone in the car."

Richard D. Bank

Max and Supa and Abe and Ida made their good-byes while the boys loaded the luggage and cartons in the rear. Lou joined his parents in the backseat as Herman slipped in between Max and Beilah. Once the car pulled out, everyone grew quiet while Max pointed out the sights along the ride. Traveling down Breed Street, Max made a turn that led into a major thoroughfare with two lanes each way for traffic and trolley tracks running down the center.

"This is Brooklyn Avenue," Max yelled over the car's rumbling engine. "You can easily catch a trolley to get you where you need to go," he said as a trolley car was approaching from the opposite direction.

As it advanced, through the trolley's front window Lou could see the conductor wearing a cap, and while it passed he saw passengers seated on benches and then another conductor in the rear collecting fares, all of which reminded Lou of being back home in Philly where he frequently hopped on trollies to take him about the city.

"There's the deli with the best lox in town!" Max pointed to a shop with the name Canter Bros in large letters spanning the width of the structure along with some Hebrew letters and a conspicuous Star of David confirming that the establishment served only kosher food.

"Enjoy the movies?" Max asked Herman, who was by his side. "If you do or maybe you just want to take a date and snuggle in the dark," he smirked as he nodded over to his left, "there's the Brooklyn Theater." Max turned off Brooklyn Avenue, made his way for half a mile, and pulled over to a corner where he parked the car. "Well, here we are. Your new home!"

The Bus Ride

Dave, Celia, and the boys gaped with eyes wide open at the three-story clapboard building on the corner demarcated by a street sign reading Marcy Avenue and Kosciusko Street. There were two stores on the ground floor, both facing Marcy Avenue, the busier of the streets. One was Weinreb's Pharmacy with signage reading Prescriptions, Drugs and Soda. Lou was pleased that soda was conveniently available. The other store was smaller with a poster taped to the window reading Grocery Store. On each of the top two floors were two front windows and two rear windows, one for each of the eight apartments.

The reverie of the four new arrivals was disrupted by Max, who thrust the car door open, leaped from the front seat, and bellowed, "Come on! Come on! Don't you want to see the apartment?"

Everyone alighted from the vehicle and followed Max around the corner to Kosciusko Street, with Lou and Herman once again trudging along, schlepping the luggage and boxes. They came to a halt at a single-frame door with peeling paint that led into the building's foyer where there was a stairway which they climbed to the third floor. Max led them down the hallway, then he stopped at the apartment at the end of the dim corridor illuminated by a single bulb dangling precariously from the ceiling. Cautiously, Herman and Lou followed their anxious parents, a beaming Max, and a smiling Beilah into the apartment that faced the rear of the building.

The door opened to a small living room and kitchen with a window overlooking the backyard. There was a tiny hallway leading to the bathroom and two bedrooms, with one that seemed to Lou to be barely bigger than a large closet. The boys dropped the baggage and stared at their chagrined parents who struggled to conceal their true feelings.

"Well? What do you think!" Max said grinning and throwing his arms in the air as Beilah gazed with a gleaming smile.

"It's more than anyone should do for us," Ceila answered, stepping up to her brother who wrapped his arms around her. "Thank you, Mordche. Thank you."

No one noticed the teardrop on Ceila's cheek.

Chapter Two
Shabbos Candles

The apartment in Uncle Max's building at the corner of Marcy Avenue and Kosciusko Street came with the basic furnishings and appliances—stove and refrigerator, double bed in each bedroom, kitchen table and chairs, sofa in the living room. The first thing the family purchased was a new electric refrigerator with an ice cube compartment cooled by freon, thus avoiding occasional gas leaks that could prove fatal. Over time, though not attaining the spaciousness and comfort of their previous residences in Philadelphia and Vineland, acquisitions here and there made the apartment feel more like home. In the living room, a cushioned chair with a footstool aside a lamp afforded a place for Dave to read one of his cherished books, most written in Yiddish by I. L. Peretz and Sholem Aleichem, which filled the new bookcase. Family portraits adorned the walls with more photos and collectibles on display atop a mahogany bureau facing the sofa and a table on which also sat a radio that brought the outside world to the Bank household. Dressers were purchased for the bedrooms; where Celia and Dave provided personal touches to their room, the boys

The Bus Ride

were left to their own devices in the room they shared. All of which was made possible by the good fortune that Celia, Herman, and Lou were able to obtain employment despite the fact the country was descending into the depths of the Great Depression.

Although the warm climate mitigated the symptoms of the tuberculosis Dave had been fighting for nine years, by late fall his condition had slowly returned to its previous state. Climbing the two flights of steps to the apartment left him exhausted and bent over the handrail, gasping to catch his breath. Sleep was intermittent as he struggled to find a position where he could be free from the aches and pain while straining to be as still as possible to avoid waking his wife. Sometimes in the morning, the sheet was damp from his night sweats, and he'd shoo Celia aside and insist on changing the sheets himself. And of course, there were the bursts of coughing often giving way to expectorations of blood and phlegm. All of which thwarted Dave's hopes of resuming work in the clothing industry.

Instead, it was Celia who became the primary breadwinner, securing a position as a seamstress in a clothing factory, having drawn from her experience helping with the family business in Vineland. Herman worked fulltime in a fruit store which not only generated a weekly paycheck but also a bag of leftover produce the owner handed to him at the end of each week along with *"a gut Shabbos."* With Lou, the question of working while in high school was more problematic than it was in Philly where he had sold evening newspapers.

Lou's territory had been on Market Street, the main east-west thoroughfare in Center City Philadelphia. The first Thanksgiving Day Parade in the country was held on Market Street, and though Lou was only four at the time, he vaguely remembered going there by trolley, feeling safe holding onto his father's hand despite being jostled and crushed by bustling bodies. Once secured in a spot close to the curb, Dave picked up his younger son by the armpits, raised him high in the air just above the heads of the other spectators and set him upon his shoulders where Lou watched wide-eyed as the parade passed.

But that was before Dave took ill, and barely six years later, Lou was hustling up and down the same sidewalks of the parade route, shouting, "Get your evening Ledger and Bulletin," while dodging automobiles and trollies as he crossed from one side of the street to the other, going where pedestrian traffic was densest. With his pleading eyes, he'd ask a passerby, "Wanna evening paper," and more often than not, the heartrending expression on the face of the boy well-recognized as a regular on Market Street at that time of day would prompt many of the prospective purchasers to fork over two cents to acquire that evening's newspaper, delivered with a smile and a thank you from the appreciative young lad.

By six o'clock, Lou had either sold all his papers or the sidewalk was deserted, but in any event, it was time to go home for dinner and attend to his homework. Lou was a bright student and had been admitted to Central High School for boys which was the only public school in Philadelphia where the criteria for admission was based

The Bus Ride

upon scholastic achievement and not geography. Though he had tried, Lou could not conceal his own excitement when, under the beaming faces of his parents, he brandished the Barnwell honor pin he received for his grade average. But the move to Los Angeles meant a new school where he had to complete his final two years.

Located in Boyle Heights, Theodore Roosevelt High School opened in 1922. The two-and-a-half-story red brick building sat surrounded by a verdant lawn with a concrete walkway leading to the imposing front doors. The school's student body mirrored the varied ethnicity of the community, with the majority of students being Jews or Mexicans, a far cry from Lou's almost uniformly white, all male, and mostly gentile classmates at Central.

But the composition of the school's pupils as well as socializing and extra-curricular activities were of little concern to Lou. He was there for the sole purpose of obtaining a high school diploma because he wanted to become a history or English teacher, and that meant college, leaving Lou with the challenge of balancing the conflicting demands between school and helping provide for his family's needs. With Lou's vocational experience limited to selling newspapers, the only job he could obtain in LA was delivering the morning papers, which required driving a car. Fortunately, the age to acquire a license in California was thirteen, and with Lou about to turn fifteen that October, he was able to secure a driver's license.

Accompanied by his dad and firmly clenching the sixty dollars in his pocket representing his savings from peddling papers and working odd jobs, Lou approached the used car lot recommended by Celia's brother, Uncle Max. Dave was never much of a businessman nor a tough negotiator. His heart belonged to the working men and women being exploited by the owners and bosses, so he was never inclined to haggle over a deal. He was a sitting duck for the used car salesman standing with his arms folded over his ample midsection and chomping on a well-gnawed stogie.

"Looking for an auto, my friend?" The bald man asked Dave, paying no attention to the wary kid at his side.

"Yes," Dave answered. "But I'm afraid we can't spend very much."

"Not to worry, my friend," the man said with a broad smile. "You can pay it out over time while we hold onto the title."

"No," Dave answered. "We pay in cash for the entire amount. This is why we can't afford...."

"Gotcha. No problem. Follow me, and if you see something you like, just point it out."

Dave and Lou trailed the man from the front of the lot to the rear as the prices on the window stickers kept dropping. Nothing was lower than one hundred fifty dollars until they reached the last row, where the man stopped.

"Ok, my friend. How about I make you a really special deal? Here's a twenty-six Ford that I can let you have for just one hundred twenty-nine dollars, and it's in great shape."

"That's more than we can afford," said Dave. The salesman frowned and bit down on his stogie.

"Well, there's not much else other than that twenty-four Chevy over there," the salesman pointed to a car with a

The Bus Ride

sticker price of seventy-nine dollars. Lou watched his dad begin to mull it over in his mind. "It has a standard transmission, three forward gears, and one reverse, and get this... a radiator and fan."

Dave was about to speak, having decided to throw in the extra nineteen dollars to close the deal, when Lou spoke up.

"Fifty," snapped Lou. The salesman glared at Lou and then cracked into a grin.

"Your kid?"

Dave nodded.

"Some fella," he smiled, twisting his lips around the cigar that he shifted to the center of his mouth. "Tell ya what I'll do. I like a smart kid. I'll let you have the Chevy for seventy dollars cash, and you drive it out today."

Lou gripped the sixty dollars in his pocket. Dave was about to say yes, but Lou spoke first.

"Fifty-five." The salesman glared again at Lou, but this time there was no forced smile.

"Sixty and not a penny lower and that's cash right now," the salesman said, stretching out his right arm with the hand palm up. Lou withdrew the money from his pocket, placed it in the exasperated salesman's hand, and bought his first car.

Neither Dave nor Lou had the foresight to question the cigar-chomping salesman about why he didn't follow through with the customary kicking of the tires, proving how sound they were. Two flats in the first week provided the answer, but other than that the car appeared to be capable of performing its duties. Every day, Lou would crawl out of bed hours before dawn to deliver newspapers. He'd return home around seven, and if it was a weekday, he'd wash up and jostle about in the tiny kitchen along with his mother and brother as they hustled to get off to work. If he had enough time, he'd sit at the table with a cup of coffee and a slice of toast while his father sat across from him reading the morning paper that Lou had brought home. By seven-thirty, he'd be out the door and off to school.

On days when Dave felt less worn out, he'd join his son delivering the papers. At first, Lou drove the Chevy while Dave tossed the papers onto their respective stoops, lawns, or driveways. But each thrust of his outstretched arm and pitch of his wrist were accompanied by a grimace and a deep breath, and by the end of the route, the papers barely made it past the sidewalk.

The next time Dave accompanied Lou on the delivery route, he headed to the driver's side of the car.

"I'm thinking, son, that maybe it would be best if I drive and you throw the papers."

Lou looked at his dad's crestfallen face and fragile grin and headed over to the passenger door. Neither spoke for a while, and after that, on those days when Dave joined Lou delivering papers, which became fewer and fewer as the months passed, Dave would do the driving and Lou pitched the papers.

After school, Lou sometimes lugged suitcases filled with newspapers belonging to the vendors selling The Los Angeles Evening Herald and Express, the new Hearst tabloid. Lou also hung around a shoeshine stand

The Bus Ride

operated by a friendly Negro man with broad shoulders, a round face, and an expansive, toothless grin whom Lou called Jim, since Jim never told Lou his last name. If a customer or two were seated impatiently awaiting their turn because Jim was busy, Lou would ask Jim, who'd be bent over the outstretched foot of a patron, if it was ok, and if Jim nodded, Lou would then shine the shoes of the man next in line, knowing he'd be allowed to keep the tip.

By the time Lou usually arrived home, dinner was being hastily set on the table by Celia and Herman. There was little conversation since everyone was pretty much exhausted and thinking mostly of getting some sleep. There was little time for studies and homework, leaving Lou struggling to pass courses let alone attain the exemplary grades he had received while at Central. But weekends were different and none more so than Friday nights, *Shabbos* eve.

Dave was an agnostic on a good day and an atheist the rest of the time. Once he stepped onto the ship that would take him to America, he never again would set foot into a synagogue except to attend a bar mitzvah of a relative. Yet, Friday night remained precious for Dave as the time for family to be together, and both Lou and Herman knew better than to make a date with a girl or play cards or hang out with the guys on *Shabbos* eve. Though Celia did not attend services, she still embraced some of the traditions such as having insisted both her sons have a proper bar mitzvah. On Friday nights, she took satisfaction spreading a white cloth on the kitchen table and inserting the Sabbath candles in the candelabra. With a caerulean scarf covering her head, Celia would light the white candles, her hands hovering over the flames as she silently recited the prayer. Pieces from a fresh challah would be broken off and distributed while Celia and the boys made the blessing for the bread. Sweet wine was poured into goblets while Dave looked on, taking pleasure watching his wife and sons recite the blessing over the wine. A special meal would follow, during which everyone would say the things they had been too weary to say during the week, and there'd be no rush to get to bed because there was no work nor school the next day. Indeed, except for Lou delivering the morning papers, it would be a day of rest for everyone, as it was meant to be.

As special as *Shabbos* eve was for the Bank family, some stood out more than others and usually because there was a guest or two present. Such a *Shabbos* occurred a few weeks into the new year of 1932 when Uncle Sam from San Diego paid his first visit. Dave and the family had not laid eyes on Sam since he and his wife, Rose, along with their daughter, Dorothy, made the migration from Vineland to California after the closure of the Bank Brothers Clothing Factory. Max was already established in Los Angeles when Sam had arrived, but he was of little help to Sam in securing a job. Eventually, Sam found work in a garment factory for men's clothes in San Diego.

Celia and the boys recited the blessings while Dave and Sam silently watched. Everyone was seated around

The Bus Ride

the table with Lou settled on a stool since there were only four kitchen chairs. Nonetheless, Lou sat as tall or taller than everyone else.

"How are Aunt Rose and Dorothy?" Lou asked of his aunt and his cousin whom he barely remembered since he was a toddler when they moved to California.

"They are fine. Next time, they will join me... or maybe all of you will pay us a visit? I understand you have a car, Lou. Nu? So, maybe you can drive your family to San Diego," Sam said with a smile spreading across his expansive face.

"Sure, Uncle Sam." Lou stood to help his mother clear the table of the empty soup bowls and serve the dinner of chicken, schmaltz, green beans, and potatoes.

"Lou's grown quite a bit since I last saw him," Sam said to Dave. "He'll be a six-footer before you know it."

Dave nodded watching Lou return with the roasted chicken that he placed in the center of the table. Though only four years apart, Dave looked like an old man sitting next to his younger brother whose smooth skin, glistening eyes, and amiable expressions exuded vigor, while Dave sat resting both elbows on the table, shoulders slumped and eyes mostly listless.

"What do you think about this Hitler and his Nazis in Germany, Sam?" Ceila asked as she seated herself.

"He'll come to power, and there'll be another war."

"Will you go to fight, Uncle Sam?" Lou asked.

"Him?" Ceila snickered. "Go on, Sam, tell the boys how good a soldier you were in the last war."

Sam squirmed before his brother came to his defense, addressing Herman and Lou.

"Your uncle came to America in 1913 and registered for the Army the very next year. No one can question his loyalty."

"And how did that work out?" Celia struggled to keep from laughing, but her twinkling eyes gave her away to her sons. This time, Sam answered the question.

"I told them I'd do whatever they wanted of me that didn't involve carrying a gun."

"You wouldn't carry a gun?" Herman asked, his eyes wide. "But isn't that what soldiers do?"

"They do other things," said Sam. "They help the wounded. They cook and wash dishes. They can relay messages through the trenches. They…"

"They mostly kill," Dave said.

"And they mostly kill, like your father said. Which is why I wouldn't carry a gun. I explained I wouldn't do anything to harm another person."

"So, what happened?" Herman asked.

"I was discharged from the Army."

"Because you wouldn't carry a gun?"

"Not just that," Celia said, smiling broadly at her brother-in-law who was also her cousin and for whom she always held a special fondness.

"There's more?" Lou gasped. Sam squirmed.

"I wouldn't salute an officer."

"Why not?" Lou asked.

"No man is above another," Sam answered, striking his fist on the table. Dave nodded in agreement, but Celia and the boys sat in silence.

"Pass the schmaltz, Lou," Herman said, changing the subject, but his uncle was not about to let the matter rest unexplained.

The Bus Ride

"This applies not just to war but to everything. To the bosses in the factories who are no better than their workers. To the bankers lending money at interest rates that break the backs of the small-business owners trying to stay afloat or a family buying a house so they don't have to live on the streets. No one is better than anyone else and certainly not because one man is richer than another man."

"And what is your solution, Sam?" Celia asked, glancing at her sons like a co-conspirator.

"From each according to his ability and to each according to his needs," Sam declared. "Please pass the schmaltz, Herman."

"So now we're back to Marx," Celia groaned.

"And what's wrong with that?" Sam retorted. "It's good enough for your friend Dubinsky," Sam said turning to his brother. "Wasn't he a member of the Bund back in Russia? And didn't he get arrested for organizing strikes?" Dave nodded.

"Who's Dubinsky, Pop?" asked Herman.

"Just someone I know."

"Go on, Dave. Tell the boys," Sam urged his brother. Herman and Lou leaned over the table, waiting for the answer, but before Dave responded Sam answered the question.

"Your father and Dubinsky met on the ship that took them both to America in 1911. Or was it 1910? No matter. They were the same age, both named David, and both from Russia seeking a better life. Dubinsky was already a socialist and active in organizing strikes, and during the voyage he convinced your father of the justness of the cause. By the time they landed in New York, they were fast friends, and when they parted with your dad leaving for Philadelphia and Dubinsky remaining in New York, they promised to keep in touch."

"Did they?" Herman asked.

"That they did," Celia interrupted. "And maybe they shouldn't have...." Celia stopped herself as her husband briefly glared in her direction, but then his face mellowed. Dave could never be angry with his wife for more than a moment.

"Ten years ago, when your dad organized a strike in Philly," Sam continued, "Dubinsky came from New York where he was already on the board of the ILGWU—"

"What's that?" Lou asked.

"It's the International Ladies' Garment Workers' Union. Your mother joined when she got her job here in LA," Sam said looking at Celia who nodded. "And now, David Dubinsky is the new president. Right, Dave?"

"Yes, Sam. And he deserves it."

"What happened with the strike Dad started?" Lou, who was not old enough to remember, asked.

"The bosses broke it...." Dave said, looking at his sons who detected a hint of fire in their father's dark eyes. "And then they blacklisted us from Philadelphia. The bastards—"

"Dave! The language!" Celia cried.

"That's why your family moved to Vineland," Sam said to the boys. "To join up with me and Max where we had opened Bank Brothers. Right Dave?"

The Bus Ride

"That's true," Dave sighed. "And now here we are, all together again and living on the West Coast," Dave said, seeking to put an end to the topic of conversation. But his brother went on.

"Nor are we the only ones coming to California. People are arriving every day from all over the country to find work here," Sam declared. "Farmers losing their farms and families losing their homes, all unable to pay the bloodsucking banks on the loans and mortgages. Men unable to put food on the table to feed their children on the miserable wages they're paid or being out of work altogether."

"It's not so great here either, Uncle Sam. I see the women shopping in the fruit store and counting their pennies and nickels to see what they can afford to buy," Herman said.

"And there are food lines out here too," added Lou. "One not far from school. If it's not long sometimes, I get my lunch there...."

"You what?" Dave raised his voice. "Don't you have enough to eat here?"

Lou slid down on his stool and stared at the table before answering.

"I don't always have time for breakfast, Pop, and...."

"Maybe this Roosevelt fellow will get things back on track," Celia said coming to her son's aid.

"He has to receive the nomination first," Dave answered grudgingly, turning away from Lou.

"Won't be enough," said Sam. "Capitalism must go. And anyway, I don't trust a man as rich as Roosevelt."

Sam paused and leaned over the table toward the boys, as far as his slight, short body would take him. Smiling he said, "And just what do you two young men think about all this talk we're having?"

Herman looked thoughtfully but was unresponsive. Glancing at his older brother, Lou spoke up.

"To be honest, Uncle Sam, I've been too busy with my paper route and picking up odd jobs and trying to do my schoolwork to have much time thinking about this stuff."

Sam slid back and slumped into his chair. Celia studied Lou, sighed, and then glanced at her husband. Dave was staring right at her, but his eyes were vacant. Slowly, a sadness enveloped his face, undetectable to everyone seated around the table but easily discernible to the woman who shares his bed.

Suddenly, a rush of chilly air swept into the room from the poorly sealed window frame just past the head of the table where Dave was seated. A spectral shadow appeared on the opposite wall. All eyes followed the line of the shadow to its source—the flickering flame of one of the *Shabbos* candles. Abruptly, the glow disappeared as the candle went out. Celia looked at her husband who was transfixed with the expired light. She fought hard to keep her tears to herself.

Chapter Three
Lou Becomes a Miracle

The winter of 1932 was the first winter the Bank family experienced without seeing a snowflake, and though there were some ambivalent feelings about this, for the most part it passed with little regret. For Celia and Dave, snow-swollen sidewalks along with biting cold held few fond memories, and while Herman and Lou recalled childhood adventures sledding down the hills in Fairmount Park and lobbing and dodging snowballs with their friends, that pleasure was eclipsed by their more recent wintry experiences peddling papers while plodding through drifting snow with their heads facedown to avoid the freezing, whipping wind. Which is why Lou relished stepping out at the break of day wearing nothing more than a light jacket during the winter months. When spring arrived and the weather warmed, he basked in the early morning sunshine on his way to school, though at times the sun's bright glare in his eyes caused Lou to sneeze, an annoyance to which he was becoming accustomed.

Hustling down Brooklyn Avenue, if he had the time, Lou loved nothing better than making a quick stop at Canter

The Bus Ride

Brothers Delicatessen. When he entered at that early hour, the tables to his right were mostly unoccupied since lunch and dinner were the main meals served. Standing behind the counters to the left were several men wearing white short-sleeve shirts with ties barely visible behind the white aprons strapped over their shoulders. Lou took a few steps toward where a juicer stood on the counter. Being a semi-regular, he was recognized by a middle-aged man with bushy eyebrows who smiled and walked over, knowing what Lou wanted—freshly squeezed orange juice, a luxury Lou had never experienced until arriving in Boyle Heights.

Lou's eyes opened wide watching the counterman grab three oranges from a bin, plunk them on the countertop, pick up the slicing knife, and slit the oranges exactly in half. Taking one half of an orange, he'd put the cut side on the plate of the strainer and bring down the hammer. In one swift motion, one hand peeled off the spent citrus and flipped it into the trash can while the other hand set a new orange half on the plate, with the process repeating itself until all the oranges were drained of their juice which was then poured from the juicer into a tall, thin glass.

Some people hated the pulp and asked that the juice be strained, but not Lou. The only thing he loved more than the pulp was the sweet, refreshing juice streaming down his throat. Not having the luxury to linger and savor the freshly squeezed orange juice, Lou would quickly empty the glass, put a nickel on the counter, head out the front door still smacking his lips, and make his way to school.

Richard D. Bank

Tentatively taking his first steps into the vestibule of Roosevelt High School three months after his arrival in LA had been like landing on an alien planet for Lou. Coming from Central High in Philadelphia, things could not have been more different. In Central, the teachers were addressed either as Doctor or Professor and were all men. Now Lou called his teachers Mister or Missus or Miss. Unlike the Principal at Roosevelt, the head of Central was addressed as President. At Central, the students sauntered through the quiet corridors, while Roosevelt's hallways reverberated with the bellows and shouts from students bustling about like a herd of cattle stampeding through a chute. But the greatest contrast between his former and current school was one that actually pleased Lou. Unlike Central, there were girls at Roosevelt High; more girls than Lou had ever seen in one place, donned in dresses or wearing skirts and blouses with puffed sleeves. Many wore trendy black Mary Jane shoes and knee or ankle socks instead of stockings.

Reflecting the general population of Boyle Heights, the girls at Roosevelt were diverse and of various ethnicities. Since almost all were Jewish, Mexican, or of Eastern European descent, most had brunette or black hair, dark eyes, and swarthy eyebrows. They looked nothing like Sally, the girlfriend Lou had left behind in Philly.

Lou met Sally at a neighborhood drugstore where she worked after school serving customers at the fountain counter. He'd sometimes stop there on his way home after selling the evening papers and have a soda. Lou could tell that Sally wasn't from the neighborhood, not with her

The Bus Ride

blond hair and blue eyes and the easygoing way about her. It wasn't love at first sight, and Lou had already known on that early spring evening when he first laid his eyes upon her that his family would be leaving for Los Angeles in a couple of months. Nonetheless, Lou and Sally fell for each other in a big way.

Lou and Sally would usually go out on their dates after she finished work at eight. They'd take a walk in Fairmount Park, which, by then, was mostly deserted since it wasn't yet summer. Lou and Sally would find some bushes, nestle in behind them, and cuddle and kiss. Afterward, Lou would take Sally to an ice cream parlor where for four cents, they'd each have a cone of ice cream. Lou loved watching Sally lick her vanilla ice cream while he bit off chunks from his chocolate ice cream. The last night they were together, each of them struggling to restrain their tears at having to say good-bye, not knowing if Lou would ever return east, Lou splurged, and they each had a hot dog and a soda which cost sixteen cents.

Standing in the foyer of Roosevelt High School for the first time in September of 1931, Lou thought back to Sally with her gleaming blond hair and bright blue eyes, and he missed her. He missed her very much.

Central and Roosevelt were fundamentally different, but then Central was fundamentally different from every high school in the country. The second-oldest public high school in the United States with demanding academic standards required to attain admission, Central was the only school in the nation able to confer academic degrees upon its graduates in addition to a high school diploma.

Lou's goal was to earn a Bachelor of Arts in English or history and then secure a teaching position or if not, proceed to college, but now this was no longer realistic. Indeed, as Lou was beginning to realize after receiving his first semester's grades at Roosevelt, college appeared less and less likely to be within his reach. Instead of all B's and A's at Central, Lou's grades were mostly C's with scattered B's and D's. Showing his first semester's report card to his parents was painful for Lou, and he turned away to avoid seeing the sadness in his mother's eyes and his father's guilt-ridden expression that his illness was to blame for all this. Celia forced a smile, telling Lou he'll do better now that he's adjusted to things, and maybe he could skip his odd jobs and Herman could pitch in with the paper route on weekends. But none of that ever happened, and Lou struggled to keep from failing courses so he could at least earn a high school diploma, if for no other reason than he knew how much it meant to his parents.

Another reason to remain at Roosevelt rather than drop out was that with public funding it provided a lunch program. Sometimes Lou missed meals, and he counted on the free lunch at Roosevelt, leaving him dismayed upon learning the government was ending the project and meals would have to be purchased. Lou was not the only student reading the poster taped to a wall conveying the news, and he couldn't suppress a "shit" from slipping through his lips as he stood in the midst of the crowd of students.

"There is an alternative," a bespectacled boy standing next to him said.

"What is it?" Lou asked.

The Bus Ride

"Aimee McPherson runs a free dining hall over on Temple Street," the bronze-skinned youth answered.

"Who is Annie McPherson?" asked Lou. The boy looked stunned.

"You don't know?" Lou shook his head. "Aimee McPherson is the greatest evangelist there is!"

"Never heard of this Annie McPherson," Lou said. Not that Lou had ever heard of any evangelists, and he wasn't sure what the word even meant. But he was hungry which made him curious to learn more.

"Her name isn't Annie. It's Aimee. And like I said, she makes more miracles than any other preacher who ever lived."

"Like what? Parting the Pacific Ocean?" Lou laughed. The boy's brown eyes seethed, and Lou regretted his comment, wanting to discover more about getting free food. "Just kidding," he quickly added.

"She heals people."

"How do you know?"

"I saw her do it at a service my parents took me to a couple of years ago," the boy explained.

"What happened?" Lou asked.

"About midway through, people started lining up below the stage. Most were in wheelchairs pushed by someone or shuffling along on crutches; some of them walked all right but had other problems like casts on their arms or being blind. Then one by one, they were brought before Aimee McPherson, and she'd lay her hands on them."

"You mean she actually put her hands on the people?" The boy nodded and continued.

"After a minute or so, she would say something about it not being her but the power of God that was inside her that was doing the healing."

"And she cured them?" The boy nodded again.

"When I was there, I saw a man throw away his crutches and hop off the stage and a young girl who was paralyzed from polio get up from her wheelchair and walk away. I saw an old lady whose fingers were all bent from arthritis, and she stretched them out so they were as straight as mine." The boy waved an open hand in Lou's face, wiggling his extended fingers.

Lou was engrossed in the story and stood staring at the boy. An idea began formulating in his mind, involving more than obtaining just a free lunch to fill his belly. He knew he had to see this Aimee McPherson evangelist person as soon as he could.

"Where did you say this place is?" Lou asked.

Having a car made it easy for Lou to get around Los Angeles, and the next day after school, he drove to Temple Street where the commissary was located. He couldn't miss the building since a growing line was extending from the entrance and down the sidewalk. The two-story structure was massive and occupied the entire block. Between the first- and second-floor windows, a signboard read ANGELUS TEMPLE FREE DINING HALL COMMISSARY, with another placard above the second-story windows reading AIMEE McPHERSON HUTTON. Lou would later learn that the surname Hutton signified her recent third marriage to the actor and musician David Hutton.

The Bus Ride

After parking the car, Lou crossed the street and milled around the crowd. Soon, he learned that once or twice a week before dinner, Aimee McPherson personally helped distribute commissary baskets filled with food and other items, including gospel literature. Lou considered bringing home a food basket, but looking at the line running down the block and around the corner, he decided it could wait until the next time. In any event, it wasn't a free meal or a food basket that he was after. It was Aimee McPherson with whom Lou wanted to speak, and he resolved to keep the following week clear of odd jobs in the afternoons and come to the Temple Commissary every day until she showed up.

Lou was disappointed that Aimee McPherson was not at the commissary on Monday and Tuesday, but he compensated by obtaining a food basket which he brought home, explaining he received it at school and only after he discarded the evangelical literature, knowing his father would go ballistic on seeing such "nonsense" and harangue against religion. But he also knew that unlike years long past when delivering such tirades, Dave would no longer breathe effusively; his eyes would no longer blare with passion; his shoulders would no longer square off with confidence; and that now, after a few minutes of great effort, he would begin to cough and cough until finally slumping into a chair. Lou didn't want to see that happen, and if there was any way he could avoid it, he would. Which is why he stuffed the pamphlets into the trash bin outside Uncle Max's apartment building before entering through the side door and climbing the stairs.

Richard D. Bank

When Lou took his place in line on Wednesday, she was there. At least that's what Lou assumed upon seeing a woman standing between two men in dark suits hovering over her while she dispensed food baskets to eager recipients with outstretched arms who genuflected in appreciation before being ushered away. But the woman looked nothing at all like the photograph in a decade-old newspaper clip Lou had been shown by Jim the shoeshine man when Lou asked if he knew about Aimee McPherson. Broadly grinning his toothless grin, Jim reached into the breast pocket of his threadbare shirt and withdrew a photo that he said he always kept there so it could be close to his heart. The lady in the photo had dark hair and a fleshy face set atop a stout body filling a plain white dress. She was seated on the armrest of a cushioned chair, balancing an open bible in one hand while her other hand was raised in the air with an outstretched finger pointing to heaven.

By contrast, the smiling, gracious woman appearing before Lou had curly blond hair with a face swathed with makeup and rouge accentuating her high cheekbones. A pearl necklace descended from her thin neck onto her exposed breastbone, and she was wearing a white silk dress that hugged her curvy figure. This woman looks more like a movie star than a female preacher, Lou thought to himself, growing nervous as he moved forward to receive his food basket.

"Next," one of the bodyguards yelled. Lou stepped up and stood across from the evangelist, who was bent facedown, drawing a basket from the table, lifting it, and then raising her head, looking directly at Lou. Smiling,

The Bus Ride

she extended the basket to Lou, who clasped it with both hands shaking.

"Thank you, Reverend McPherson," Lou said, unsure how to address this woman who was the most famous person he had ever met, which made him feel that Mrs. Hutton wouldn't do.

The evangelist smiled, saying, "Just call me Sister Aimee. And what is your name, may I ask?"

To Lou her voice rang out like the church bells he would hear resonating on Sunday mornings when delivering papers. The evangelist leaned closer to Lou and studied his features, which she took to be handsome, and she was particularly impressed with his neatly parted hair and innocent blue eyes.

"Lou Bank," he answered. Sister Aimee's penciled eyebrows drew together as she examined Lou further, trying to discern his ethnicity since his name provided no help.

"How old are you?"

"Eighteen," Lou lied, which he often did when asked his age. His height and mature demeanor made it easy for him to be convincing. "Rev... er, Sister Aimee, can I ask you a question?"

"Of course, you may."

"Do you think there might be some work I can do here?" he said, although Lou had more in mind than just a job. Sister Aimee swiftly shifted from her cheerful expression to a serious deportment as she again drew her eyebrows together and appraised the young man before her. Slowly a smirk surfaced on her lips.

"I don't think there's anything here for you…" Sister Aimee paused, almost taking perverse pleasure in the downcast expression on Lou's face, before she hastily added, "but I do have something in mind." Sister Aimee smiled watching Lou perk up. Withdrawing a card and a pen from her purse, she wrote upon the card on which her named was imprinted and slid it across the table to Lou.

"You know where the Angelus Temple is, don't you?" Lou nodded though he had no idea. "Be there Saturday at noon and give this to one of the ushers at the entrance." Lou took the card.

"Thank you. I'll be there…." Before Lou could say thank you once more, he felt a pair of sturdy arms push him along, making room for the next supplicant.

That Saturday after delivering the morning papers, Lou went home, showered, shaved, dressed in a fresh short sleeve shirt, slacks, tall socks, and his two-toned brogue shoes.

"You have an afternoon date?" Dave asked, looking up from the Yiddish newspaper he was reading as his son slipped past him, heading for the door.

"Sort of," Lou sheepishly smiled, not wanting to discuss his true objective.

"Have a good time," Celia called from the kitchen.

Lou had mapped out the route to his destination which would be taking him through parts of LA where he had never been. The Angelus Temple was located in Echo Park which was northwest of Boyle Heights. He'd be driving through downtown LA and then go past Mission Junction, Dogtown, and Angelino Heights—names all foreign and

The Bus Ride

strange to him—but his car was sound and he foresaw little likelihood of breaking down in one of those places. Nonetheless, it wasn't until entering Echo Park and, according to the map, being only blocks away from Angelus Temple that Lou's tight grip on the steering wheel eased and his knuckles faded from bright red to crimson and then to their customary pale shade.

Driving slowly and scrutinizing the unfamiliar surroundings, Lou's eyes expanded when out of nowhere arose the most awesome vision he had ever seen. Looming over him was a colossal cross perched atop a massive concrete dome coated with a mixture of ground abalone shells that served as the roof of a four-story circular structure, reminding Lou of the brickwork stadium at the University of Pennsylvania which ran the length of a city block where he had peddled programs at Saturday afternoon football games. But this building was constructed in bright concrete with doorways on the ground floor and windows at the upper levels. He easily imagined it as a Roman colosseum like the one he had seen in his schoolbook when studying Latin at Central. But there would be no clashing gladiators inside this edifice which Lou presumed to be a house of worship and a place of peace and tranquility with a serene atmosphere for quiet contemplation—a world apart from the small synagogues and tiny, raucous *shuls* he was familiar with. Or at least so Lou thought after parking his car and making his way to join the throng slowly flowing through the entrances.

Reaching an entryway, Lou withdrew the card that Sister Aimee had given him from his pants pocket and handed it to the attendant. The man studied it for a moment, raised his head to scan the area around him, and then yelled, "Peter!" The named man was quickly upon them.

"Pete, take this," said the attendant, handing the card to a middle-aged, pallid-faced man wearing a dark suit, white shirt, and tie. "You know what to do."

"Follow me," Pete said gruffly to Lou. Turning on his heels, Pete tunneled through the crowd, leaving Lou hustling to catch up. With Pete elbowing his way down one of the teeming aisles, Lou followed and kept looking up in amazement at the dome painted azure blue with fleecy clouds, making Lou feel he was actually gazing at the sky. Returning to ground level, all Lou could see were rows and rows of seats forming a semicircle before a sprawling stage with a podium in the center. Lou estimated several thousand people were already seated with almost as many places remaining to be filled. The clamor was jarring, and it was with relief that Lou followed Pete up the stairs to the stage and then into a room backstage where the racket finally subsided.

The room wasn't much bigger than the bedroom Lou shared with Herman, and it was so dark that even if Lou hadn't been wearing sunglasses, it still would have taken a while before his eyes adjusted and he could make out the contents. In addition to a chair and two wheelchairs, the walls were covered with an assortment of objects hanging from hooks: crutches, canes, arm casts, leg casts, metal leg braces, head bandages, back braces, and even a couple of stretchers leaning against one wall.

The Bus Ride

"I see you're wearing sunglasses, so I guess you're supposed to be blind," Pete snickered. At first, Lou thought the man was joking and he smiled back, but when Pete kept staring at him, Lou felt compelled to answer.

"No. It's just that it's a sunny day...."

"Ok," said Pete. "You'll just be blind in one eye, and we'll leave it at that. Makes for some variety anyway. Grab one of those canes, and keep your sunglasses on and wait here," Pete pointed to the chair. "Someone will be back for you in about half an hour. Meantime, you can leave the door open and watch..." Pete stopped himself and sneered, "I mean *listen* to the program."

With that, Pete spun on his heels and was gone, leaving Lou alone in the room. Lou was puzzled as he gazed around the room once more, removing a black cane from the wall and then seating himself on the chair.

Before long the stage filled with men and women attired in the way Lou had observed families dressed when promenading to church Sunday mornings. Some were seated while others stood, and soon the massive auditorium was infused with the soothing melody of a Kimball pipe organ. In a short time, the stage was packed and all the seats in the amphitheater occupied. Abruptly a roar arose from the multitude, accompanied by applause and cheers and screams. Lou's eyes shifted to the stage where a pathway surfaced in the sea of those assembled the way Lou imagined the waters must have parted for Moses. But this was not the Hebrews dashing from the shoreline of slavery to the shoreline of freedom that Lou was witnessing. Rather, it was a celestial corridor arising from somewhere behind the towering curtains and advancing at a steady pace until reaching the pulpit at center stage where Sister Aimee emerged in all her glory wearing a flowing white gown with a lustrous cross suspended from a silver chain upon her pearl-white chest.

For the next fifteen minutes, Sister Aimee preached, but Lou had no idea what she was saying since he was unable to hear a thing past the shouting, whooping, and swooning from the people prancing, swaying, and fainting in the hall and the thuds of bodies dropping on the stage and in the aisles in response to shrieks of, "Drop it like it's hot!" Every so often, thousands of arms hoisted in the air, emulating the thrust of Sister Aimee's right fist reaching for the heavens, followed by more screeching and squealing at her every exhortation. Lou had never witnessed such pandemonium and grew exhausted just watching.

Suddenly a man appeared who looked and dressed just like Pete but who was not Pete. The man grasped Lou by the elbow.

"Your name?" Lou was puzzled. "Your name? What's your name?"

"Lou."

"Fine, Lou. Come with me, and just keep that cane swinging side to side and tapping the floor in front of you." Seeing the bewildered look on Lou's face, the man quickly added, "Look kid, it's all right. You're like a warm-up act to get the crowd going. Nothing more, and when it's over, you'll be taken away and you'll get to see Sister Aimee."

The Bus Ride

Lou did as he was told, excited at the prospect of speaking with Sister Aimee. As soon as Lou and the man who looked like Pete stepped onto the stage, a hush swept over the auditorium, and Lou slowly followed his escort while swaying his cane as instructed. Straight ahead he spied Sister Aimee staring directly at him with glowing eyes and a bright, welcoming smile, seeming to Lou to be the closest thing to an angel he had ever seen. When Lou was no more than a few feet from the podium, the man who was not Pete grabbed him by the shoulder and held him in place while Sister Aimee spoke.

"And whom do we have here?" Sister Aimee addressed Lou's escort.

"We have Brother Lou who cannot see in one eye and hardly at all in the other."

Sister Aimee stepped out from behind the dais and firmly laid a hand upon Lou's shoulder as the man who looked like Pete but was not Pete released his grip.

"Do you believe, Brother Lou?" Lou nodded. "Do you believe in the power of God that is within me to heal you?" Lou nodded again. "Say this for all to hear, brother."

"I do!" Lou bellowed.

"Remove your glasses, Brother Lou," said Sister Aimee, and Lou complied.

"Look out at your brothers and sisters in the audience. Can you see them?"

Lou was a quick study and knew what to do. Blinking, he peered at the enthralled throng of thousands, gradually raising his eyelids until the whites of his eyes bulged to the point that some seated in the front rows feared they might explode in his head. Heaving his arms in the air and turning to Sister Aimee, whose scarlet lips had burst into a jubilant smile, Lou yelled.

"I can see! I can see!"

Swiftly, scores of people spilled into the aisles, many on crutches or in wheelchairs, some limping along with the aid of canes, of whom many were polio survivors; others were blind and guided by a friend or family member. There were even folks joining the procession who appeared healthy but suffered from a myriad of ailments: hearing loss, arthritis, injuries, cancer, heart conditions, and other infirmities. But despite the varieties of their illnesses, each and every man and woman, boy and girl making their way to the stage sought healing from the hands of Sister Aimee, who would in each and every instance maintain that it was not her but God working through her that combined with their faith in the Lord's power to heal, would cure them.

Abruptly, Lou felt fingers firmly grip his shoulders, swing him around to face backstage, and push him along at a hurried pace. The pair zigzagged their way through a maze of curtains, props, harried crew members, and darkened corridors. Suddenly a clang resounded in Lou's ears as a steel door was thrust open by the man steering him who looked like Pete but was not Pete. Lou stumbled into the bright sunlight that despite his sunglasses, temporarily blinded him. Trying to keep up as best he could, Lou followed his guide to a building adjacent to the rear of the Temple where the man stopped to catch his breath, allowing Lou to do likewise.

The Bus Ride

"Here we are," the man gasped, gazing at the building.

"What is this place?" asked Lou.

"It's the parsonage," Lou's escort said. Lou had no idea what that meant which the man discerned from Lou's expression. "It's where Sister Aimee lives," he added.

Lou studied the semicircular, stucco building surrounded by a four-foot concrete wall atop which wrought iron latticework had been installed. Between the gates leading into the compound and the structure within was a magnificent lawn and gardens easily accessible from the residence by half a dozen glass doors spaced equidistant on the dwelling's first floor. On the second level, numerous floor-to-ceiling windows with wrought iron latticework and narrow concrete slabs were spread out on the façade.

"Let's go," the man said, taking a deep breath and leading Lou to the front door which was opened by an elderly, stooped man wearing a black suit with a low-cut white waistcoat, reminding Lou of the butlers in the mystery movies he had seen, some of whom turned out to be murderers.

"Here, kid," said the man who looked like Pete as he handed Lou a small envelope. "So long," he added, turning on his heels and walking off muttering something under his breath that Lou could not quite make out but sounded like *good luck* followed by a chuckle.

"This way," muttered the elderly, hunched man leading Lou through a center hall with a vaulted ceiling, up a stairway to a corridor, and into a room with bright sunlight shining through a window overlooking the gardens.

Richard D. Bank

Stepping gingerly into the chamber, Lou stopped and gaped at the finest furnishings he had ever seen. White wicker chairs formed a semicircle by a window and around a wicker table on which sat a glass vase filled with flowers. Chairs and small tables with more vases and flowers were placed in the corners of the room. In the center of the room was a plush, floral upholstered, sphere-shaped sofa so huge that it occupied the remainder of the area.

"Make yourself comfortable," the old man leered revealing crooked, yellow teeth as he closed the door behind himself on his way out.

As soon as the door shut, Lou withdrew the envelope from his pocket and opened it to see a crisp five-dollar bill. Given the brief time spent and such little labor involved, Lou considered this to have been the best paying job he ever had, but it was more than money he was seeking. Folding the envelope and slipping it in his rear pocket where it fit snugly and could not fall out or be pickpocketed, Lou sat himself on one of the soft-cushioned chairs overlooking the verdant lawn and blooming gardens with their profusion of white, red, and yellow blossoms. The fragrance of the flowers in the vases filled his nose, almost causing Lou to sneeze. The sun no longer surged into the room but was at an angle barely trickling in, leaving much of the chamber in a shadow. Lou's eyelids grew heavy, and he struggled to stay awake. He'd been up since four, and so much had happened since then.... Lou fell asleep.

Entrenched in a deep slumber, Lou was mostly unresponsive to the stroking he was beginning to feel on his shoulders, but when it became a shaking accompanied by

The Bus Ride

laughter, Lou quickly woke up, and his eyes widened at the amused face of an angel only inches away. Bolting from his chair, he barely avoided knocking over Sister Aimee, but she backed off just in time. Lou stood sputtering as his face turned bright crimson while he retreated from the woman who looked even more beautiful than she had onstage.

"I… I'm sorry…."

"No need!" Sister Aimee laughed. "You earned it. Helping to heal the sick can indeed be tiring. And you did a fine job facilitating the process for so many brothers and sisters to be cured today." Sister Aimee detected a puzzled expression on Lou's face.

"Oh, I can see you're confused. It works this way," Sister Aimee sauntered closer to Lou and did not stop until he could feel her breath on his face and smell the alluring fragrance of her perfume. "No one wants to be the first person to be healed since good Christians are taught to be patient and give preference to others. You know, 'the meek shall inherit the earth'…."

Sister Aimee paused, waiting for Lou to acknowledge that he understood, but nothing was forthcoming from Lou because he hadn't a clue what she was trying to get at or what she meant by being meek and inheriting the world. Sister Aimee took a deep breath and continued her explanation.

"That's why we have someone like yourself come up first… to get things started."

"So, all those other people really are sick?" Lou asked, feeling relieved because if the whole thing was just a sham, then his mission was already a failure.

"Of course, they are," Sister Aimee said. "I know there are skeptics, and that's why the First Baptist Church conducted a survey of thousands of people who came to me. Do you know what it showed?" Lou shook his head. "It showed that eighty-five percent reported that over time, they were completely or partially cured through me."

"So, you heal them?"

"No, I don't heal anyone." Lou knitted his eyebrows, puzzled. "I am merely the medium through which the power of God works the cure," sighed Sister Aimee, raising her eyes toward heaven.

"How is that done?" Lou asked. Sister Aimee stepped even closer to Lou, and he felt her gown brush against his legs.

"I'll show you…. But it's so warm in here…." Sister Aimee stepped away to one of the windows and lifted it, permitting a breeze to enter. She then strolled to a closet in the far corner of the room, turned, and addressed Lou, saying, "Let's make ourselves more comfortable."

Lou didn't understand what she meant and stood spellbound as she opened the closet door, slipped out of her gown, and hung it up. Lou blushed, having no idea what was going on, but he did feel a throbbing in his crotch at seeing Sister Aimee wearing nothing but a shiny silk chemise trimmed with lace.

"Aren't you going to get a little comfier too?" Sister Aimee asked.

"I… I'm fine."

"Well," Sister Aimee shimmied over to Lou. "At least let's take off your shirt so I can show you how I heal

The Bus Ride

people," Sister Aimee said, staring into Lou's eyes while her bare thigh brushed against his leg. Slowly, she began undoing his buttons.

"Sister... Sister Aimee," Lou stammered, "I'm not so sure about this. Suppose your husband comes in? He'll get the wrong idea..."

"Oh, that won't happen," Sister Aimee laughed, backing away and placing her hands on her hips defiantly. "I'm divorcing that fat pig! Do you know how he's introduced at the beginning of his cabaret act with all those half-naked women on stage parading around? He's called Aimee's Man! How do you think that makes me look? The swine has no morals! I didn't know it at the time, but when we were married last year, he was already engaged to another woman! Know what she's doing now?" Lou shook his head. "The harlot's suing him for breach of promise. That's what! And it's in all the papers!"

Lou felt his face flush and knew it must be turning crimson again. Though relieved there would be no confrontation with a jealous spouse, Lou still felt uneasy with what was going on, but he was helpless to move as his feet seemed cemented to the floor. Sister Aimee resumed her composure and drew even closer. Lou could hear her breathing intensify while she tugged off his shirt.

"It begins with the laying of hands," Sister Aimee spoke softly, sounding more like a songbird than someone serving as a conduit through which God was about to work a miracle. Lou felt Sister Aimee's supple hands rest on his shoulders.

"Do you have faith, brother?" Lou made no reply. "You must have faith for God to heal you."

Lou remained unresponsive, not knowing what to say.

"Maybe you need a little help," Sister Aimee breathed into his ear. "I'll just have to lay my hands on other places...."

Lou sensed Sister Aimee's fingertips all over his body: floating about his neck, fluttering down his chest, alighting on his stomach, stopping at his waist, undoing his trousers.

What happened from that moment on, though mostly a blur, was at the time and for the rest of Lou's life one of the most exceptional experiences he ever had. The only thing he specifically remembered was tumbling with Sister Aimee onto the massive circular sofa. Once landing on the divan, Lou felt he was in the midst of a revival service with himself embodying the entire congregation and Sister Aimee as the spirited preacher.

Her movements were frenetic; her lips, tongue, fingers, feet, and thighs were everywhere, flying in the air, enveloping his all too willing torso that responded with a mind of its own. One moment she was under him and then above him and then entangled with him while her exhortations and shrieks bounced off the walls, resonating with cries of "Praise be to Jesus!" and "Have faith in the Lord!" and culminating in a barrage of "Oh God, Oh God, Oh God!!"

Finally, as if reacting to the cries of "Drop it like it's hot," the refrain Lou had repeatedly heard during the service, Sister Aimee collapsed on Lou, leaving her bare breasts straddling his sweaty head.

The Bus Ride

Lou had no idea how long he and Sister Aimee remained entwined, lying naked on the couch and half asleep, but it wasn't until the room grew dark as the remnants of sunlight pierced the windowpane and surrendered to dusk and a cool breeze chilled their bodies that they began to stir. With nothing expressed other than sighs of satisfaction, Lou and Sister Aimee dressed—Lou more hurriedly and she more leisurely. Lacing his shoes, Lou broke the silence.

"Sister Aimee, there is something I would like to ask you."

"Go ahead," Sister Aimee said walking over to the window, closing it, and drawing the curtains after switching on a lamp. "I have a bit of time left, though not much. Seems I've been here longer than planned," she coyly grinned, drawing up a chair and sitting across from Lou.

"It's my dad. He has TB. Can you heal him?" Lou blurted.

"I'm sorry to hear that. How long has he been ill?"

"Ten years."

"How bad?"

"Bad. And it's getting worse. We moved here from Philadelphia for the warm weather, but now the winter has him back to where he was when we left last summer. Maybe he'll improve… but I don't know…."

"Tell me, my brother, has your father accepted our Lord and Savior, Jesus Christ?"

Lou looked into Sister Aimee's bright eyes and knew he must speak truthfully.

"We're Jewish." The answer didn't seem to faze Sister Aimee.

"Does your father have faith in God?" Again, Lou felt he had to be honest.

"No. My dad doesn't believe in God and has nothing to do with religion."

"Then I'm afraid there isn't anything I can do for your father," Sister Aimee said, stretching out her arm and resting her hand on Lou's knee. "As I always say, I cannot heal anyone. The power to heal comes from the Lord and can only be received by someone who has faith in the Lord."

"Can you at least try?" Lou asked.

"It would be pointless." Seeing Lou slump his shoulders and his face turn desolate, Sister Aimee offered an option. "How about if you bring your father to a service, and perhaps he will receive the Lord and become baptized and then we can see about a healing?"

Lou looked up and saw the sincerity in Sister Aimee's eyes. She seemed to truly believe in what she was saying, though from what he saw that day at the Temple and then the fling on the sofa, he had his doubts. But none of that mattered because Lou knew his dad would rather die than submit to what Sister Aimee would require of him. Dave was honest and didn't have a hypocritical bone in his body which made Lou proud of his father. He could never ask him to be anything else.

"I thank you for the offer, but I'm afraid not, Sister Aimee," said Lou rising from his chair. "I really need to go now."

Sister Aimee stood and watched Lou walk to the door.

"Keep the faith, my brother."

"I'm afraid I don't have that kind of faith to keep, Sister Aimee," said Lou. Opening the door and turning back, he added just before stepping out, "Guess I'm just like my dad."

The Bus Ride

Lou's chest filled with warmth and pride as he closed the door behind him.

Chapter Four
Lou's Left Alone

The summer of 1932 marked a full year since Lou's family had migrated to Los Angeles. In that time, they acclimated to the Boyle Heights neighborhood and grew comfortable in their apartment, making the most of every nook and cranny while covering the walls and filling the shelves with family portraits, personal mementos, and Dave's thirteen-volume collection of Sholem Aleichem's books, none of which Herman nor Lou could read since they were written in Yiddish. When not working, time was shared with extended family members at their homes or in parks and occasionally at the beach.

While Dave's condition did improve somewhat with the warm weather, he was still unable to work, but Herman and Celia held full-time jobs, and with no school until September, Lou let it be known he was looking for something to augment his newspaper route. Hearing of this, Uncle Max stopped by the apartment one evening and made Lou a proposition.

"Want to make some extra money, Lou?" Max asked, plopping on the chair Lou had carried from the kitchen to the living room so his father's brother had a place to sit.

The Bus Ride

"Sure would, Uncle Max," answered Lou, glancing at his father who was settled in the armchair and leaning into the conversation with interest.

"It's Saturday's and Sunday's, and you'll be away overnight," Max said, catching his breath from climbing the stairs and mopping the sweat from his brow with a handkerchief.

"But what about your paper route, Lou?" Dave asked, becoming uneasy about this new job.

"I can get someone to cover for me, Pop. What do I have to do, Uncle Max?" Lou asked.

"As you know, I'm a fruit merchant," Lou nodded. "Well, given these times when so many businesses and people don't have cash, transactions are often made by bartering. You know what that is, don't you?"

Lou nodded again, though he wasn't exactly sure what it entailed.

"So, what I'm doing is trading oranges for chickens."

"Why would you do that, Max?" Dave asked, growing intrigued. "Everyone loves oranges, and people buy them here all the time."

Max looked at his younger brother and smugly smirked, lowering his voice as if they were all co-conspirators and he was disclosing a plan to break into a bank.

"That's just it, Dave. Here in LA, the only thing we have more of than people who love oranges are the oranges themselves. We have more oranges than we know what to do with! Do you know how many are thrown away at the end of each day?" Lou and Dave shook their heads. "Thousands and thousands. But in some places, there are hardly any oranges, and people living there love oranges just as much as we do."

"Like where, Uncle Max?"

"Salt Lake City."

"In Utah?" Dave said.

"Yes. In Utah. What I do is send my oranges to Salt Lake City where I can get a much better price than here, but with the Depression and so many people and businesses without cash, they can't afford to pay. So, instead of money, I take chickens!"

"Chickens?" Dave said incredulously.

"And what do you do with the chickens, Uncle Max?" Lou asked, dismissing his father's skepticism.

"I eat them!" Lou's eyes widened in disbelief. Uncle Max laughed at his nephew. "No, Lou, I'm just kidding. I don't eat them. I sell them here where there aren't enough chickens to feed the people who want to eat them. Some I sell to the kosher butchers and some I sell to the *goyish* butchers—whoever pays best. And they pay in cash!"

Lou and Dave nodded their heads, clearly impressed.

"Now, Lou, what you have to do is before dawn on Saturday, pick up the truck that's been loaded with oranges and drive to Salt Lake City, stopping only for gas and relieving yourself. That way, you'll be there by midnight."

"In one day?" Dave asked. "How far is it?"

"Six hundred miles but it's easy on a weekend. Almost all open roads and little traffic."

"What about eating, Uncle Max?"

The Bus Ride

"Have your mom pack some sandwiches and fruit. And bring a thermos for coffee to keep you awake. You can get drinks and refill your thermos when you stop for gas."

"Max, I can't let my son do this. He's not even sixteen...." Dave coughed and slumped back in his chair; his face filled with despair.

"Look at him, Dave," Max said, sizing up Lou who was standing by his father. "He's practically a grown man. And a tall one at that!"

"Where do I sleep, Uncle Max?"

"You can pull off the road when you get to the farm and sleep in the truck. It'll be nice and cool at night. Better than sleeping in a hot apartment in the summer," Max added, looking around the windowless room and mopping his forehead again with his handkerchief. "Before sunup, they'll unload the oranges and stuff the truck with chickens, and you'll be on your way back by eight and home by midnight."

"What does Lou get paid for all this, Max?"

"Seven dollars and fifty cents. And gas money, of course."

"Only seven-fifty?" Dave murmured.

"My brother, this is a good-paying job. It takes thirty driving hours, and at twenty-five cents per hour for sitting and driving a truck, I can get fifty men with wives and kids to feed begging to take it. But I want to help my own family first."

"Fine, Uncle Max. It's fine and thank you." Lou knew that he wasn't getting more than the federal minimum wage, but the family could certainly use the extra income. "When do I start?"

"'This Saturday, Lou. Come by Friday afternoon, and I'll give you the key to the truck and money for gas since I'll be in *shul* on *Shabbos.*"

Dave rolled his eyes and bristled that while his brother was in synagogue praying to God and promising to be a good and righteous Jew worthy of God's benevolence, he was paying his own nephew seven dollars and fifty cents to spend an entire weekend driving 1,200 miles and sleeping in a truck. But what could Dave do? He looked on wearily watching Max stand with a broad smile on his face and shake Lou's hand, sealing the deal on the weekly trips to Salt Lake City to exchange oranges for chickens that Lou would undertake in the summer of 1932.

Summer passed swiftly, and in September Lou returned to Roosevelt High, retaining his paper route and working odd jobs. As the fall wore on, Dave's health continued to deteriorate. Despite the weekday morning turmoil with Celia and the boys navigating their way around each other in the bathroom, clanking about the kitchen grabbing dishes, utensils, glasses, milk, juice, coffee, bagels, toast, and cereal, and the noise from the banter, conversations, and hushing each other to be quiet, Dave remained in bed, hoping to compensate for fitful nights without much sleep. When he finally did haul himself out of bed near noon, the apartment would be empty, leaving him alone and no longer feeling constrained for the sake of his family to control his hacking and the spewing of scarlet phlegm.

In the bathroom, along with washing himself, Dave would examine his pajamas, and if he spotted a bloodstain, he'd use warm water and soap to clean it, hanging the

The Bus Ride

garment to dry and removing it from the rack before his wife returned from work so she wouldn't see it. Breakfast and lunch coalesced into one meal that Dave was barely able to ingest. Clenching the daily paper and a book, he'd plop into his armchair and read, dozing on and off, until the first of his family would arrive home before dinner.

Such were Dave's days, one mostly indistinguishable from another, with the prospects for an improved future not in sight. Indeed, his condition grew even worse with the onset of chilly winter nights, and it was on one such Friday evening at the end of January that Dave made his announcement.

Like every *Shabbos* eve, the family was seated at the kitchen table covered with the white tablecloth reserved for Sabbath and holiday dinners. Father and sons watched Celia put on her headscarf and light the candles while reciting the prayer and fluttering her hands over the flickering flames. Herman, who had a natural talent for singing, chanted the blessings over the bread and wine while Lou passed around portions of challah, and everyone lifted their glasses and sipped the sweet red wine. The Sabbath rituals concluded, Celia set the candelabra on the counter and headed to the stove to fill bowls with chicken soup.

"Celia, please sit, I have something to say before we eat," said Dave.

Celia looked at her husband with alarm, recognizing that the tone in his voice was usually reserved for matters of serious concern. She did as she was asked without saying a word. Dave nodded his appreciation. They had been married long enough that silent communication between the two was second nature. Dave gazed around the table and then spoke.

"This coming Monday morning, I will be leaving for Philadelphia."

"What?" Herman shouted.

Dave's eyes settled on his elder son, but he said nothing.

"Where will you stay?" Herman asked.

"I'll be living with my mother and sister."

"There's no room for you, Pop, not with Bubbe Tuba, Aunt Celia and Uncle Joe, and their kids," Herman said.

"There will be enough room. I only require a sofa and a chair." Dave glanced at Celia. Their moist eyes fixed upon each other. Nothing more need be said between the two of them. But more explaining had to be done to satisfy the boys.

"Why can't you stay here?" Lou asked.

I'm a burden, and it breaks my heart seeing the three of you having to watch me suffer, Dave wanted to say but did not.

"I'll be able to get more care from Bubbe Tuba. She has nothing much to do but help with Celia's kids. Celia doesn't even let Bubbe cook except for *Shabbos* and holidays. This way she'll feel useful."

"But we can take care of you here," Lou pleaded.

"I know you can, but in Philadelphia, I'll have someone to help me all the time. Mom and your brother work, and you have school and your paper route. Here, I'm alone all day, but living with my mother and sister, I won't be alone. It's only temporary, Lou."

The Bus Ride

Celia braced her back, fighting to control the trembling in her body, understanding all too well the double entendre in what her husband had just said.

"As soon as you graduate, you'll all come back home, and we'll find a new place to live with the money the three of you will have saved." Dave forced a smile, peering at his wife for confirmation.

Herman and Lou stared expectantly at their mother, trusting an honest response would be forthcoming that would convince her husband to abandon this plan. But unlike Dave who was not difficult to read, the boys did not detect the glint of despondency in Celia's eyes exposing the guise of someone resigned with having to lie.

"Yes, it makes sense," Celia said, addressing each of her sons in turn. "We'll work and save and return to Philadelphia and move to an even bigger house than the one we had in Vineland. You'll have graduated high school, Lou, and can go to college. After that, you'll make so much money you can pay for your brother to take singing lessons so he can become a famous singer!" Celia smiled at Herman, the only member of the family who did indeed possess a melodious voice.

"It's settled, then," proclaimed Dave. "The Bank family has a plan." Dave sighed in satisfaction. "Now, let's eat."

Without a word being spoken, Dave, Celia, Herman, and Lou all shared the fear that this could be the last *Shabbos* meal they would ever partake in together again.

The winter of 1933 was the most awful of Lou's young life. Even worse than the winter a decade earlier when his father first became ill with TB—his body wracked with aches and pains, his chest throbbing from constant coughing, his hair matted and skin soaked from night sweats. And then the time the doctor was summoned after Dave collapsed during the family seder, leaving the boys terrified at having to watch their father strapped to a stretcher, carted down the steps by two men in white, thrust into an ambulance, and sped away to the hospital.

In many respects, the winter of '33 adhered to the same routine as previous months. Celia, Herman, and Lou went through all the motions fulfilling their respective responsibilities. On weekdays, Celia and Herman went to work and Lou to school after completing his paper route. Weekends, the boys picked up odd jobs and Celia attended to the housekeeping. But no matter where Celia or the boys positioned themselves in the tiny apartment, they could not escape the barren air permeating their living quarters nor could their eyes avoid the vacant chair in the living room and the shelves devoid of Dave's books, reminding them of the pervasive void in their lives.

There were letters back and forth between husband and wife, father and sons, and the phone call on Friday nights, a desperate attempt to retain the family ritual of past years. But there was no way to avoid noticing the increasingly wobbly handwriting in Dave's missives and the mounting weakness in his voice. On one Friday night in mid-March, it was not Dave at the other end of the line but his sister, Celia Yusem, telling her sister-in-law that Dave's condition had continued to deteriorate and perhaps they should come home.

The Bus Ride

Preparations were quickly made, and by the following Friday, the apartment had been emptied of their belongings; Celia and Herman had given notice at work; suitcases and bags were packed; and two tickets were purchased to take the train to Philadelphia—one each for Celia and Herman but not for Lou.

"You must stay here and finish school."

"But Mom..." Lou pleaded.

"Your father and me, we both insist."

"But I may have to take some classes in the fall to graduate."

"Then you will. Arrangements have been made. You can stay with Uncle Abe and Aunt Ida as long as you need...." Celia's voice broke seeing the anguish wash over her son's face and envisioning the suffering in the dark eyes of her husband whom she'd soon see.

Lou knew there was no use arguing as he picked up two suitcases and trudged down the stairs to where he and Herman would pack everything in his car. He'd drive his mother and brother to the train station, make a tearful good-bye, and then drive himself to the house where he would live with his aunt and uncle.

After living two years in Boyle Heights, Lou knew his way around as he drove from the train station that Friday evening to his new residence, which he could not even begin to consider being a home without the presence of his parents and brother. The sun was setting when he reached the tree-lined street where black wires strung taut on poles loomed over the treetops. Almost all of the stucco ranch houses had potted roofs and fenced-in front yards. Lou recognized his aunt and uncle's home, having visited many times with his family, so there was no need to check the house numbers while he parked his car. Gripping a suitcase in one hand and carrying a bag in the other, he used his hip to swing open the gate. Lou stopped to gaze at the house, fighting back tears welling in his eyes. What Lou really wanted to do was turn around, run to his car, and drive all the way back east without ever stopping. But he did not. Taking a deep breath, Lou knocked on the door.

Living with Uncle Abe and Aunt Ida, whom Celia's brother frequently called Chaika, was relatively easy. Abe was the first of the family to migrate to California in 1920 and well settled in his home and job as a tailor, or more precisely a "waist maker," in a clothing factory. Ida was a housewife, and since she and Abe did not have children, she had both the time and the inclination to be exacting in keeping her abode free of clutter with a precise place for everything. Which presented a bit of a problem since unlike Herman who was meticulous in his demeanor and neatness, Lou was on the untidy side and appeared sometimes disheveled. His failure to immediately return an item to its assigned spot or put the newspaper in the reading basket or rinse his dishes before Ida would wash them with soapy water caused his aunt to raise her bushy eyebrows and cluck her tongue. She'd glare and frown until Lou would restore the offending object to where it belonged or clean up what was messy or stuff his shirt into his trousers or do whatever it took to get his aunt to grudgingly signal her approval with the cessation of her tongue clucking.

The Bus Ride

On the bright side, Aunt Ida had plenty of time to cook, and she took pleasure in having another mouth to savor her culinary skills. Lou was rarely around for breakfast or lunch, but he usually partook in the dinners, wolfing down Aunt Ida's specialties: blintzes and sour cream, brisket with mashed potatoes awash in gravy, kreplach served in soup, kasha varnishkes, stuffed cabbage, and best of all, her special dessert of kugel made with noodles, fruits, and nuts. Lou indulged himself with second servings, having no pangs of guilt doing so since he figured it was a fair trade off, given that the amount he paid for room and board consumed all the money he made from his paper route, leaving him with what he earned from his odd jobs for pocket money, cigarettes, and taking out a girl for a soda and ice cream or maybe to a movie.

Despite all the delectable dishes Lou enjoyed, his taste buds were most tantalized at the crack of dawn when he was between his paper route and heading off to school and all by himself in his uncle's verdant backyard. Aunt Ida and Uncle Abe would not yet be up and about when Lou would open the back door, feel the breath of fresh air sweep against his face, squint at the rising sun, and sneeze. Lou would then cross the small patio and step onto the lush, green lawn, making his way to the leathery-leaved evergreen trees bearing the oranges Lou loved. There wasn't much time remaining in the growing season—just through June for navel oranges—so Lou took advantage of the opportunity almost every day to snatch a few from one of the trees, carry them back to the kitchen, cut each in half, and squeeze them on the juicer. He'd pour the contents including the pulp into a glass, swigging it slowly. The juice quenched his thirst, and the pulp satiated his stomach, and the taste satisfied his soul. Lou was set to start the day, and such was his new routine until Sunday, June 11th when it abruptly came to an end.

With no school on Sundays and the shoeshine stand closed, after delivering the morning papers, Lou generally went back to bed and slept till noon unless he heard guests in the house or noisy neighbors in adjacent yards or he would be struck by the glare from the sun's beams streaming through the windowpane. But this time, he was awakened by a persistent knocking on his door which opened before he could arise. Remaining behind the door with just their heads sticking through were Uncle Abe and Aunt Ida, sharing frowns and sadness that instantly caused Lou alarm.

"Lou, you'd better get dressed. Your uncles Max and Sam want to see you," said Abe.

"Sam? He's here from San Diego?" Uncle Abe grimly nodded. "Where is he?"

"At Max's house."

"When do they want to see me?" Lou asked, sitting up in bed.

"Now. They say it's important, Lou," Ida said with an unaccustomed warmth in her voice.

"What is it? Is everyone OK in Philly?" Lou leaped from the bed, beginning to unbutton his pajama shirt, prompting Ida to blush, turn on her heels, and walk away while Abe let out a sigh but said nothing more before following her.

The Bus Ride

In ten minutes, Lou was out the door and in his car driving to Uncle Max's house which was also in Boyle Heights. The stucco ranch houses on the street where Uncle Max lived were similar to those from where Lou just came, except the lots were slightly larger, the houses a bit bigger, and the foliage less abundant since the area was recently developed. Lou leaped from his car and ran up the path leading to the porch of his uncle's home. Though the door was partway open, allowing fresh air to pour in the house, Lou knocked and waited while catching his breath. The door opened all the way, and Aunt Supa stood before him, her glasses balanced on the bridge of her nose and her lips parting, allowing a slight smile. Pleasantries were briefly exchanged as she led Lou through the living and dining rooms and to the back door leading to the rear yard. Opening the door, Aunt Supa nodded at Lou who stepped out on the patio where his uncles were seated, both wearing short-sleeve white shirts and fedoras to shade themselves from the sun.

"Have a seat, Lou," Max said, pointing to a lawn chair opposite them. "How are you?"

Ignoring the question, Lou quickly sat.

"Uncle Abe said you wanted to see me and that it was important," Lou said, trying to control the pounding in his chest. Max glanced at Sam before taking a deep breath.

"I received a telegram from your mother last night, Lou. It seems that your dad, and our brother," Max looked at Sam again, "has taken a turn for the worse."

Lou felt his insides in turmoil, and he braced himself before speaking.

Richard D. Bank

"How bad is it?"

"Your father's dying, Lou. I wish I didn't have to tell you this. He wants to see you before he goes."

Tears surged in Lou's eyes. He pictured his father's withered torso contorted in the throes of coughing convulsions, fighting to stay alive so he could look upon his son one last time and speak his final words.

"You must leave immediately, Lou. No time to waste."

Lou looked at his Uncle Sam who was nodding with teardrops dribbling down his cheeks. Max pulled himself up from the chair, reached into his pocket, and withdrew some cash. Lou and Sam also stood, with Lou looming several inches over his uncles.

"Here, Lou. This is thirty dollars for a bus ticket to Philadelphia." Lou gazed at the outstretched hand and then at Uncle Max and reluctantly took the money.

"But it'll take six days by bus, Uncle Max, and it's only three days by train. It may be too late...." Max said nothing. "Can't you get me a train ticket? I'll pay you back as soon as I can... I promise...."

Max fidgeted but remained silent. Lou looked beseechingly at Sam who averted his eyes, unable to face his nephew. Finally, Max spoke.

"It's all I can afford, Lou. I wish I could do more. You know, Lou, after your mother and brother returned to Philadelphia, it was left to us," Max glanced at his brother for confirmation, "and your mother's brothers, Abe and Max, to be responsible for you."

"I've paid my own way, Uncle Max. Uncle Abe gets all that I make from my paper route...."

The Bus Ride

"Not nearly enough, Lou," Max smiled patronizingly.

Lou was furious. He knew Max could easily afford the price of a train ticket. Lou turned toward Sam with his eyes pleading. Sam reached into his pocket and pulled out some bills before bending down to remove a leather jacket hanging over a chair.

"Here's six dollars for food, Lou, and take this jacket to keep warm. Nights can be cool in some parts of the country even this time of year."

Lou knew there was nothing more to be gained. He accepted the money and the jacket, shook hands with his uncles, and promised to contact them when he reached Philadelphia. Rather than going through the house, he ran around the yard and out to the street, jumped in his car, and drove off, figuring out what needed to be done to get on the road as fast as he could.

First thing Monday morning, Lou was at the principal's office, and he explained the situation to the receptionist, a middle-aged, heavy-set woman with round glasses, curly, graying hair, and a polite but condescending attitude. On learning of his father's condition, she hurriedly murmured, "I'm sorry to hear that," while withdrawing from a drawer a form that she slid across the desk.

By 11:00 that morning, Lou had secured the signatures of all his teachers approving his withdrawal thus ensuring that a grade for each course would be provided at the end of the term, which was only a week away. The document indicated Lou would return in September to take the remaining courses needed to graduate.

Lou then drove to the distribution center where he received the papers for his morning route and informed the cigar-chomping manager, who still didn't remember Lou's name, that he had to go back east. The manager grunted and couldn't have cared less, knowing a hundred others would jump at the job. Lou then drove to the Greyhound terminal on South Los Angeles Street where he purchased a ticket for early the next morning to go to Philadelphia. Lou slipped the three ten-dollar bills Max had given him over the counter and received the ticket.

After two years living in Los Angeles, it took only a few hours to do what was necessary to leave it all behind. Despite having more than his share of dates, there was no special girlfriend for Lou to say good-bye to like there had been in Philly when the family moved west. He knew some guys at school and in the neighborhood to hang with, play cards, and once in a while, do things they shouldn't be doing like drink liquor and shoot craps for money, but like the girls he took out, there was no one he would miss nor would any of them miss him. Lou mulled all of that over on the drive to Abe and Ida's.

That evening, the mood was somber, with Lou barely touching the farewell dinner of brisket and mashed potatoes that was his favorite. When Lou broached the subject of Dave's condition, his aunt and uncle squirmed and cast uneasy glances at each other, saying they knew only what Lou had relayed from his meeting Sunday morning with his two uncles. After dinner, Lou packed all his belongings in one suitcase, thankful that he would not need a warm set of clothing upon arriving in Philadelphia. After looking

The Bus Ride

around the room, opening the drawers and checking the closet, making sure he had all that he intended to take, Lou walked into the living room where Abe and Ida were sitting.

"Uncle Abe, this is for you," Lou said, handing his uncle a sheet of paper. "I signed the car over to you. Can you sell it for me?" Uncle Abe nodded. "Keep half of whatever you can get, and send the rest to me."

"No need for that, Lou. I'll wire you the full amount."

"Please. I'd rather have it this way. You and Aunt Ida went out of your way to have me here. Please...." Abe looked at his wife who shrugged.

"If you insist, Lou."

"Just one more thing," said Lou. "Can you go with me to the bus depot in the morning? We'll have to leave at five."

"Of course," said Abe.

It was still dark when Abe and Lou slid into the '24 Chevy. Lou tossed his suitcase onto the rear seat. It was too early for much traffic, and they arrived at the Greyhound bus depot with time to spare for Lou to catch the 6:00 bus heading east. Lou left the key in the car and removed his suitcase from the back.

"So long, Uncle Abe. And thanks again for having me." Lou extended his hand which his uncle grasped.

"Have a safe trip, Lou. Please tell your mother that Ida and I are thinking about her." Abe said nothing about Dave which miffed Lou since his father was not only Abe's brother-in-law but also his cousin, but the thought was fleeting since Lou had much more on his mind.

Lou stepped out of the car with the suitcase in one hand and the brown leather jacket in the other.

"Have a safe trip," Abe shouted. Lou did not look back as he entered the lobby of the bus depot.

PART TWO

The Bus Ride
June 13-19, 1933

Chapter Five
Lou Takes a Chance

Lou squinted and then sneezed at the ascending sun's rays glinting off the shiny metal of the bus he was walking toward. This was the vehicle scheduled to transport Lou to St. Louis where he would board another bus with Philadelphia as its final destination. Lou knew it was a Greyhound from the backward running canine painted on the letterboard and the bus's etched crown of another dog and the words Greyhound Lines. On the other side near the top of the bus, the phrase "Coast to Coast" was inscribed. Lou observed several Black men strapping luggage to the roof. He stopped and waited until he saw his suitcase being secured before he walked to the front cab where the bus driver stood.

Lou stopped in his tracks, overcome by an unsettling queasiness. There was something familiar about the bus driver... Lou struggled to make a connection. Suddenly it struck him that the man bore a remarkable resemblance to the men marching in the newsreels that preceded the movie features where he often took his dates. Stomping with their arms thrust forward in the air and their legs stiffly lifted off the ground, they were accoutered much

The Bus Ride

like the bus driver who was clad in a uniform with a Sam Brown belt strapped around his waist and across his chest and wearing knickers and boots. Lou worried that the driver might be a compatriot of the marching men, who had crooked necks and eyes focused upon a platform where a similarly attired man with a tiny, square mustache above his lip was viewing the spectacle with satisfaction. Lou had learned from his aunt and uncle that the man on the podium was Adolph Hitler, the new chancellor of Germany.

"Hitler's nothing but a Jew hater, Chaika... he'll be worse than the Czar!" Uncle Abe spat, looking up from his paper while Aunt Ida glared, giving the evil eye to the heavens, demanding that the Nazi leader be struck by a bolt of lightning from above. And since no one could summon a curse like Aunt Ida, Lou kept checking the papers and the newsreels at the movie theaters for word that the German chancellor was dead. But that didn't happen. There were only more parades.

"Ya getting in, kid?" the bus driver said, warily eyeing Lou.

Lou examined the driver more closely and discerned that unlike the helmets worn by the marching men in the newsreels, the driver was wearing a livery cap sitting at a slight tilt on his head. Nor was there any sign of a Nazi insignia on his uniform. With the seats beginning to fill and the bus driver growing impatient, Lou proceeded to the open door, nodded at the driver, and stepped up and into the bus.

The seats were mostly occupied as more passengers worked their way down the aisle, and Lou feared he might be forced to take the solitary seat behind the driver, about whom Lou still had lingering doubts. There were eight rows with two seats on each side of the aisle, and though Lou preferred a window seat, at this point, he'd take anything. When Lou reached the last row with two empty seats on the right, he slid through and plunked down on the one by the window. Lou folded the brown leather jacket and propped it up as a pillow on which he rested his head. Listlessly, he turned to gaze at the sun rising on the horizon of a cloudless sky.

Lou's mind filled with details of the trip, pushing aside for the moment the ever-present dread that he wouldn't make it in time to see his father before he died. Lou knew the first stop with something to do other than eat, drink, piss, and gaze at the barren vista was Reno, Nevada, about 500 miles away, where the bus would arrive sometime late Wednesday afternoon. After that, except for Kansas City, the following three days would have little to offer other than staring out the window until reaching St. Louis, where he'd board the bus taking him to Philadelphia. If all went as scheduled, he'd be home at the break of day on Monday, June 19th.

The big problem, his growling stomach reminded him, was that he only had six dollars to spend on cigarettes and food. Cigarettes were just fifteen cents a pack, and he could likely panhandle a glass of water or a cup of coffee. But there wasn't much leeway when it came to food at the small eateries and lunch counters along the way, with gas pumps situated out front, where breakfast usually cost two bits, lunch four bits, and dinners at least seventy-five

The Bus Ride

cents. Lou was always good at numbers, and it didn't take a genius to quickly calculate that something had to go. Despite his head being filled with the trip's expenses and whether or not his father would still be breathing by the time Lou reached him, Lou allowed his worries to slip away and his eyelids to droop while his body eased into a well-deserved repose.

Lou had no idea how long he had been asleep when he felt an elbow brush against his ribcage, awakening him from a sound slumber. He shifted in his seat, turning away from the window where the sun had risen so high in the sky that it was no longer visible. Glancing at the elbow firmly implanted on the armrest and following the arm up to the shoulder and then to the neck, Lou studied the face of the passenger next to him. Thick black hair swathed the scalp while swarthy brows drooped over dark eyes. The man's mouth was partly open, baring a fine set of white teeth as he looked straight ahead, apparently lost to the world with nothing or perhaps everything on his mind as he sat comfortably in the seat which provided plenty of space for his slight torso. Lou wondered if his traveling companion spoke any English, not that he cared much one way or the other. At that moment, the man became aware that Lou was awake.

"Have a good sleep? You were dead to the world."

Lou nodded, thinking, *the Chinaman speaks English*. He sat up, stretching himself and yawning.

"You must have been quite tired." Lou nodded again. "Well, you'll have plenty of time to rest and sleep before we get to Reno," the man smiled. "My name is George. George Kuwa."

"Lou Bank." Lou extended his forearm, and the two shook hands. "Nice to meet you," said Lou.

"What is your destination, Lou?"

"The end of the line—Philadelphia."

"That is some distance. May I ask what takes you so far?"

"It's my hometown. Been in LA for two years and now heading back." Lou didn't want to talk any more about his return, so he asked the same question of George.

"Reno. That's it for me. I'll stay a night or two and then return to LA." George grew silent and studied Lou, who was staring at him. "I bet you're looking at me and wondering if you know me from somewhere. Right?"

Not really, Lou thought to himself. George looked like every other Chinaman he'd seen, and there were many in LA. He never could distinguish one from another unless he got to know one well.

"I don't think we ever met," Lou finally answered.

"We haven't. But you may have seen me, nonetheless." Lou appeared puzzled. "Ever see any of the Charlie Chan movies?" Lou nodded. "Any of the silent ones?"

Lou shook his head. George seemed disappointed but then brightened up.

"Well, if you had, you would have seen me!"

"You were in a Charlie Chan movie?"

Lou was becoming interested in his traveling companion. Lou loved going to the movies where the lights went out, leaving everything pitch black except for the

The Bus Ride

white haze generated by the projector and the illuminated screen, which Lou could only see if he crooked his neck since he almost always sat in the front rows. Lou would lose himself in the world emerging before him for a couple of hours until he could almost hear the film flapping in the projector's reel, and the lights would go on as the screen grew dark.

"What was your part?" Lou asked. George flashed a mischievous grin.

"Charlie Chan, of course," George answered smugly.

"No way," said Lou, his mouth gaping.

George nodded, smiling broadly. Lou stopped to think.

"Well, I guess it makes sense to get a Chinaman to play a Chinaman, although now it's some white guy."

"But I'm not Chinese."

"No?"

"I'm Japanese." Lou wasn't that surprised. He knew he wasn't the only one who couldn't tell the difference between one Chinaman and another nor distinguish a Chinaman from a Jap or a Korean.

"Which Charlie Chan movies were you in?"

"Just one." Lou looked disappointed. "But it was the most important one of all," George said, preening like a peacock.

"Why?"

"Because it was the first. *The House Without a Key* in 1926. Not a big part, but it was the first time Charlie Chan appeared on the screen, and I was the one playing the role!"

"Wow," was all Lou could muster, thinking maybe he should get this guy's autograph.

Richard D. Bank

"You know, I made almost sixty films up until two years ago, but my favorite role was Chan." George gazed out the window, seemingly lost in thoughts of what might have been. "Unfortunately, the movie wasn't successful, and I was replaced by Kamiyama Sōjin when they made *The Chinese Parrot*, but that didn't go well either, and the role was then given to a Korean named Park in the next film."

"Did anyone Chinese ever play Charlie Chan?"

"No. Sōjin was Japanese like me, and Warner Oland, a white Swede, played Chan in *Charlie Chan Carries On*, which became a hit."

"Why no Chinamen?"

"You don't know?" George looked at Lou, wondering how he could be so naïve. "If you haven't noticed, my young friend, white people are not so keen on us yellow people, and that goes double for the Chinese."

"The Chinese?"

"Yes. Ever hear of 'The Chinese Exclusion Act?'" Lou shook his head. "Well, what do you think it means?" Lou cocked his head, giving the matter some thought.

"Sounds like it keeps out Chinese people."

"Yea. That's pretty much what your country did about forty years ago, and for me, it turned out to be a good thing."

"How's that?"

"Left lots of room for cheap labor when I came here in 1907 when I was twenty-two. Jobs were hard to come by in Japan, and since I was not the first born who inherits everything, like my older brother, I had little prospects other than going abroad where I could get work and make enough to live on and save, so I could return home with

The Bus Ride

a nest egg. I was lucky because the year after I arrived, the United States forced Japan not to issue passports to the U.S. except for women marrying U.S. citizens. Like I said, Americans don't care much for the yellow race."

Lou was dumfounded at what George was telling him. He knew a number of Asians in Boyle Heights, and most of them seemed OK, and he enjoyed the occasional dish of Chinese food he'd eat. In school he was not taught about these laws against allowing the Chinese and Japanese into the country.

Yet, he fully believed what George was saying since he knew from the stories he'd been told about his own family and how bad conditions had been for the Jews in Russia, and though while an improvement, things were still difficult here. Lou had more than his share of catcalls hurled his way about being a dirty Jew or a Christ-killer or a kike. Indeed, Lou concluded early on in life that prejudice and worse were part of the landscape of living. He didn't need to be informed about bigotry and persecution from a Chinaman or a Japanese guy. But Lou loved movies, and he wanted to hear more from George about that.

"How'd you get into making pictures?" asked Lou.

"Purely by chance," George grinned. "I often got day work on Pathé Studios' lot in Culver City. One time when I was carting boxes from one set to another, an assistant to the director ran up to me, saying they needed a Chinaman for a scene. The rest is history!" George let out a hearty laugh, and then his face grew gloomy. "But I'm finished with pictures now...."

"Why did you stop?" George's eyes darkened, and he answered in a sober tone.

"Because I died." Lou's forehead furrowed. He had no idea what George was talking about. Then Lou's eyes brightened, and he laughed.

"Hey! You had me for a minute there. Really, what happened?" George shook his head, and his demeanor deepened even more.

"I'm not joking, my friend. There is a death certificate on public record showing that in 1931, George Kuwa died of natural causes while asleep in his boarding room."

George stared intently at Lou who was squirming and growing uncomfortable with the way the conversation was going. He began to consider that maybe this George *Koowah* person wasn't an actor at all and never played Charlie Chan in a film and was just some crazy guy sitting in the last row of a bus heading to Reno, and maybe Lou shouldn't let himself fall asleep until they got there.

Sensing his traveling companion was becoming leery, George thought the time had come to share his well-kept secret about the entire story and devious scheme, since in a few days, he'd be on his way back to Japan anyway.

"Now, I'm going to tell you something that I haven't told anyone if you promise to keep it to yourself at least for a week." Lou solemnly nodded. "It's like this. In the first three Charlie Chan films, Chan was a minor character, and the movies were not successful nor much remembered. In 1931, when Fox Films made Chan the main character in *Charlie Chan Carries On* and it was

The Bus Ride

a hit, they didn't want any of the Asians who previously played Chan to go around bragging about their roles."

"Why not?" asked Lou. George looked at Lou as if he was an imbecile.

"You don't get it, do you?" George said. "Most Americans hate Asians."

"Why?" Lou asked.

"Who knows why?" George threw up his hands. "Why does any group of people hate another group? Maybe it's because Chinese and Japanese immigrants worked hard when they got here, and many became successful. Or maybe because they took jobs away from white people. Maybe because we just look different. I don't know...." George shrugged. "But hate us they do. Do you know we are called the Yellow Peril?"

Lou shook his head. George stared at Lou and sighed.

"Well anyway, the people at Fox knew it wouldn't be good for the box office if Charlie Chan had his origins in Asian actors, so they arranged with Universal, which produced the second Chan film, to keep Sōjin's mouth shut, which they could do because they had him under contract. There was no problem with Park staying quiet because Fox produced the third film and had him under contract as well. Which left me, and believe it or not, I never had a contract with Pathé. It was just a small part that no one imagined would ever amount to much, and they were in a rush to get the scenes shot. I was paid the next day and never bothered going where I was supposed to go to sign the contract. I didn't care whether I had a contract or not, and no one ever followed up. But because of that, I was free to do and say as I wished about my role in the film." George settled back in his chair and smirked, savoring the words he was about to speak.

"I agreed to stay quiet about playing Chan, but it cost Fox a pretty sum. I was willing to sign an agreement, but they didn't trust me, and they wanted something more than a potential lawsuit to hold over me to maintain my silence."

"What was that?"

"They killed me off. Just like getting rid of an unwanted character in a script. I died." Lou was dumfounded.

"What do you mean you died? You're sitting here next to me." George laughed.

"Yes, that's quite right. I'm here, but legally, George Kuwa is dead. The studios in Hollywood are powerful, and it was easy to have all the paperwork filed to kill me. There's the death certificate I told you about. They put a small obit in the papers. I have no driver's license and no identification. All the Fox people have to do is make an anonymous call, and I'd be deported in an instant. I could probably stay here for a while longer, but my plan was to go home once I made some real money, and now I have, and I'm hoping to add to the pot in the next day or two with my visit to Reno. But win or lose, I'll be on a ship next Monday heading back to Japan with enough stash to live comfortably."

Lou looked at the man seated next to him in a new and admiring light. As he studied George Kuwa closer, an idea began to percolate in Lou's mind.

"Suppose you lose in Reno?" Lou asked.

The Bus Ride

"Well, first of all, I don't intend to lose, and if I do, I'm only playing with a small portion of my money. But I'll win. I usually do!" George laughed.

"How do you do that?" Lou asked. George crinkled his forehead, staring at Lou.

"Why do you want to know? You don't look like much of a gambler to me," George said, sizing Lou up. "Are you planning on some gambling during the holdover in Reno?"

"I don't know.... Maybe."

"Well, the game I play is roulette. Familiar with it?"

Lou often watched craps and poker and sometimes took part when he had spare change, but roulette was something he only heard of and saw a couple of times in the movies.

"A bit," Lou answered, not wanting to appear inexperienced.

"Then you know what the table and wheel look like. The betting can be very complicated, so I suggest you keep it simple. If you want to go for a long shot with a high payout, place your bet on a single number. Otherwise, you're best to stick with betting on odd or even, red or black, even units of numbers like one to eighteen or nineteen to thirty-six."

"Thanks," Lou said, processing the information.

As the bus sped on, George and Lou settled into their seats. George closed his eyes, but Lou was wide awake while he conceived a solution to suppress the persistent rumbling in his stomach.

With the exception of a pit stop for gas where Lou left the bus to go to the restroom, relieve himself, wash up, and buy a cup of coffee and a doughnut, Lou remained seated even when the bus reached a luncheonette. He spent the day gazing out the window, dozing on and off, and sometimes talking with George about the movies his traveling companion had been in, several of which Lou had even seen. By the time the bus pulled into the parking lot of a diner with the sun slowly setting in the horizon, Lou was famished. He jostled down the aisle, hustled over the asphalt, and burst through the diner's entrance, securing an available seat at the counter where he ordered and subsequently devoured a bowl of chicken soup, meat loaf and mashed potatoes swathed in gravy, a slice of cherry pie, and coffee. On the way out, Lou bought a pack of cigarettes, quickly peeling off the foil, removing and lighting one, and inhaling deeply while still savoring the meal.

But as the bus drove off, contentment gave way to uneasiness as Lou subtracted the cost of his indulgence that left him with four dollars and six bits, and the knowledge he couldn't manage on that over the remaining five days. Lou could only see one solution to his dilemma, and he resolved that he'd do what had to be done. His mind made up, Lou fell into a deep sleep, not waking until the next morning when a new bus driver looking almost exactly like his predecessor and wearing the same style uniform was at the wheel announcing they'd be in Reno as scheduled by the end of the day.

As the bus steered into the Greyhound station on Stevenson Street, most of the passengers were busy gathering their belongings since Reno was their journey's end.

The Bus Ride

After coming to a stop and opening the doors, the bus driver stood and addressed the passengers with what sounded to Lou like a memorized speech.

"Welcome to Reno, Nevada. Reno offers two things that no other state in the country can: legalized gambling enacted in 1931 and divorce laws passed in 1927 allowing a man or woman to obtain a divorce after six weeks of residency. Most of the visitors are here for one or the other—to win a fortune or dump a spouse." The bus driver weakly smiled amidst scattered chuckles.

"Now, if you are disembarking and have luggage stored, please line up along the side of the vehicle to claim your belongings after they're removed from the roof." Lou looked out the window and spotted several Black men bustling over to the bus. "If you are continuing on, please be back before eleven o'clock when we will be promptly departing. Until then, feel free to enjoy what Reno has to offer. There are many fine restaurants and gambling halls only a few blocks away. And a word of caution, don't let the eighty-degree temperature fool you. Once the sun sets, it can drop into the fifties."

Grateful for the leather jacket Uncle Sam had given him, Lou grabbed it and rose from his seat along with George. The two men stepped into the aisle, waiting for the line to move forward.

"Well, Lou, nice meeting you. Have a safe trip going east." Lou and George shook hands. "Are you going to try your luck here?"

"I might."

Richard D. Bank

"Well, if you do, I'll be at the Palace, and should you wind up there, look for me at the roulette table and I'll buy you a drink." George smiled and ambled along with the line exiting the bus.

By the time Lou stepped off the bus, except for those retrieving luggage, the passengers had dispersed onto a swarming Stevenson Street. Just a block away, Lou sighted a congested thoroughfare with cars parked diagonally along both sides of the wide avenue. Upon reaching the roadway, Lou saw an arch stretching at least thirty feet above the ground and spanning from one side of the street to the other. At the top of the arch, in letters as tall as Lou, the word RENO was displayed and below in letters half the size, appeared the phrase: THE BIGGEST LITTLE CITY IN THE WORLD. Bulbs installed to illuminate the arch suddenly flickered but cast little light with the sun still descending on the horizon. Lou figured the arch would glow brightly enough at night, and he could easily sight it should he lose his way.

Lou hadn't eaten all day, and in addition to the gnawing in the pit of his belly, he began to feel lightheaded. Seeing a placard over the door of a small establishment across the street identifying it as a sandwich shop, Lou figured he could get something not too costly to appease his hunger. He crossed the thoroughfare, entered the eatery, and after perusing the menu, he ordered a burger, French fries, and a cup of coffee, which after buying a pack of cigarettes on the way out, left Lou with little more than four dollars. Mulling this over in his mind, Lou knew he had only two options. He could interrupt his trip in St.

The Bus Ride

Louis and make some extra money by picking up odd jobs. No one was better than he at securing such work. Then he could continue to Philly. But that would delay seeing his dad which was out of the question, so Lou knew he really had only one course of action available. He felt for the four dollar bills folded in his pocket, looked up at the dark sky and then at the glare of lights coming from a tall structure not far off. Like a moth drawn to a flame, Lou walked in the direction of the building.

Approaching the illuminated intersection teeming with cars and people, Lou couldn't believe his eyes. The four-story edifice that seemed to have mysteriously summoned him blazed brightly with letters running down from the roof to the second floor and another set of letters above the entranceway identifying the building as the BANK CLUB. Lou was convinced this was no coincidence and nothing short of a miracle guaranteeing that he would find good fortune, enabling him to continue his trip uninterrupted and with a full stomach. He would not be greedy, he promised himself, and once he doubled his money, he'd return to the bus terminal. Lou remained wide-eyed as he passed through the open glass doors and below a placard proclaiming the Bank Club as the largest licensed casino in the United States.

Lou felt as if he had been set adrift in an expansive sea teeming with people, mostly men in fedoras or bareheaded and almost all wearing coats and ties. Lou quickly slipped into his leather jacket. He wasn't exactly sure what a roulette table looked like, but he soon found himself in the midst of patrons clustered around tables where huge wheels with staid-looking men wearing visors stood in the center. Seeing the numbers on the tables and wheels, Lou knew he was at the right spot.

Lou spent the next half hour peering over the shoulder of a bald, corpulent man in a brown suit who never budged while his belly pressed against the table filled with small piles of what looked to Lou like checkers but everyone called chips. Lou observed that after each spin of the wheel, the chips would quickly change hands, with the man wearing the visor reeling in most of them more times than not and then dispersing a portion to unsmiling recipients. This puzzled Lou since he pictured himself breaking into a wide grin if he received extra chips from the man with the visor, and yet almost everyone around the table wore subdued expressions, win or lose.

Just when Lou felt he had the lay of the land, the fat man heaved a hefty sigh, swept the trickle of chips remaining in front of him into his flabby hands, and stepped away from the table, enabling Lou to swiftly take his place. Lou withdrew the four dollar bills from his pocket, set them on the table, and before he knew it, the man with the visor replaced them with a small stack of chips. Lou was now ready to double his money.

Lou's strategy was simple, just as George had advised. He would place a chip on each of the safe bets of one through eighteen and nineteen through thirty-six and a chip on the riskier bets with bigger payoffs bearing the numbers eighteen and thirty-six, thus playing four chips with each spin of the wheel. Selecting these numbers was not difficult since as long as he could remember, the

The Bus Ride

number eighteen and its multiples were auspicious numerals for Jews—something having to do with the Hebrew word for life since Hebrew letters also denoted numerals, and the letters spelling life likewise stood for the number eighteen or something like that. In any event, Lou was convinced that given the gaming establishment bore the same surname as his and for all he knew could be some long lost relative from Russia, and Lou was betting on numerals that were practically holy, how could he lose?

In less than ten minutes, Lou found himself staring in disbelief at the empty space on the table where his chips had once been piled. It all happened so quickly that he had no recollection of any bets or sliding chips onto numbers or the results of each spin of the roulette wheel or the man wearing the visor taking away his chips followed by Lou replacing them at the same spots. All Lou knew was that except for some small change remaining in his pocket, his money was gone, and he had a five-day bus ride ahead of him with no prospects for procuring any nourishment. The only consolation was that given his struggle to keep himself from throwing up on the roulette table, wanting to eat was the last thing on his mind. Lou was broke and in a serious bind, and he knew it when he felt a heavy tap on his shoulder and smelled the fetid breath from a man with a moustache and sneer on his face saying, "C'mon kid, move on. You're done for the night."

Lou was in a daze, bobbing like a buoy in an ocean of bodies as he bounced from one to the other until he staggered out the door. Along with his four-dollar bankroll, he seemed to have lost his sense of direction, unsure which way to go. Fortunately, he remembered to look for the arch with Reno brightly illuminated. Swiveling his head, he spotted the dazzling letters, and he stumbled toward its glittering message, the Biggest Little City in the World. Fifteen minutes later, Lou was at the Greyhound bus station, making his way from the entrance on Stevenson Street through the dimly lit terminal and out the rear door, where his bus began filling with mostly solitary figures shuffling down the aisle and slipping into seats generally at a distance from one another.

Lou had no desire to sit closer to the front, which would have made it easier to exit at the stops along the way. All he wanted to do was to return to the rear of the bus and slump onto the window seat of the last row on the right where he began his journey, go to sleep, and not wake up until he found himself in Philadelphia where he'd race as fast as he could into his father's arms.

Chapter Six
Alma

Lou did not feel the thrust of the bus pulling out of the depot nor smell the fumes spewing from the exhaust pipes through the partly open window nor hear the engine churning as it accelerated along the streets of Reno and then onto the highway. Lou was sound asleep and remained so until the sun's rays blazed through the windowpane. Wearily raising his eyelids, he quickly shut them but not soon enough to avoid sneezing in the direction of the radiant orb. Lou stretched his arms then quickly withdrew them, not wanting to inadvertently strike the passenger next to him. He looked over but the seat was empty, so he spread out. Lou gazed around and saw that both seats across the aisle were likewise vacant and scanning the front, no more than half were occupied with the closest passenger across the aisle and a row up. Lou's stomach grumbled, and he was grateful no one heard. Suddenly, he was startled by the booming voice of the bus driver.

"We'll be reaching Salt Lake City close to noon, folks, right on schedule for a two-hour holdover. I know it's been a long haul, so feel free to have a meal, walk about, and

The Bus Ride

take in the fresh air. There'll be a new driver taking you to Denver. Have a safe trip."

Lou sagged into his seat, wishing he could disappear. Why even bother getting off to stretch my legs, Lou thought to himself. That would only make him even more hungry. Lou knew he could manage for a day without eating—he had before when fasting on Yom Kippur. But no way could he go for five days without any food at all. He knew he had to make a buck someway, but how? He pondered the possibilities: beg, borrow, or steal? Swipe a tip left at a food joint? Look for forgotten change in a phone booth? Check under the seats for something dropped?

Having quickly dismissed stealing, he was still mulling the other options when the bus pulled into a fairly full parking lot with a huge sign reading, COVEY'S NEW AMERICA MOTEL & COFFEE SHOP. In the center of the site stood a single-story, white-framed building with a peaked, red roof and signage reading coffee shop, while situated along the parcel's perimeter were several two-story, colonial-style brick buildings designated by another large sign publicizing 200 hotel rooms with air conditioners, radios, and telephones.

Coming to a halt, the driver opened the door and barked a reminder to be back by two. Lou sulked and watched while the fifteen or so passengers began filing out. He turned facing the window and stared at the traffic and a sign reading Main Street.

"Why aren't you getting off to have something to eat?" Lou looked up at a woman hovering over him. Lou thought she might be the passenger seated on the other side of the aisle and one row up, but he wasn't sure. Lou sat erect.

"Not hungry." Lou half smiled.

"I don't know how that can be. I don't see a lunch box on your lap, and we've traveled four hundred miles with just two brief stops, so how can you not be hungry?" The woman conversed in an articulate tone reminding Lou of several female teachers he had at Roosevelt who frequently displayed the same air of concern as did the woman standing before him.

Though she was not much past thirty, the woman looked old to Lou but most everyone that age looked old to Lou. She appeared to have a fine figure, but it was hard to tell from the wide-shouldered, mid-calf-length dress she wore. Lou liked her Greta Garbo slouch hat that covered most of her head, leaving only a Marcel wave of straw-colored hair visible. The woman remained silent, contemplating Lou with penetrating green eyes that made him feel he could tell her most anything and so he did— almost. Lou told her about not having enough money for the cross-country trip and then losing it while trying to win more. The woman stared at Lou for a moment, and he figured she'd leave now that her curiosity was satisfied. But she didn't.

"I would like you to have breakfast with me.... What is your name?"

"Lou."

"Ok, Lou... Will you join me for breakfast? My treat." She smiled.

The Bus Ride

Lou couldn't see the harm, and in any event, he was too hungry not to accept. It wasn't costing him anything though he'd soon find out there was a price to pay—there always is.

"Thank you."

"I'm Alma." The woman waited for Lou to stand before she turned to walk down the aisle. Lou followed.

The bus was parked near the entrance to the coffeehouse, where the counter was already mostly occupied and all the tables taken, but Alma and Lou were able to secure a booth by a window facing one of the red-brick buildings. Alma and Lou spoke sparingly while perusing the menu and placing their order. Alma selected ham and eggs with toast lightly buttered while Lou ordered a stack of pancakes and bacon though he was hungry enough to order more, but he did not want to appear gluttonous. Alma requested a pot of coffee and two cups, dismissing the hassled waitress with a genteel nod.

"So, Lou, tell me about yourself," Alma said, folding her hands on the table and leaning forward expectantly. Lou fidgeted, not sure how to respond. "How old are you?"

"Eighteen. I'll be nineteen in October," which was the month of Lou's forthcoming seventeenth birthday.

Alma remained reticent, clearly seeking more. Lou squirmed.

"Can I have a cigarette?" Alma pulled a pack from her purse, offered one to Lou, and withdrew one for herself, handing the matches to Lou who lit both cigarettes. "Thanks."

"I'll buy you a pack on the way out. Now, other than returning to Philadelphia, I know nothing about you. Do you work? It's so hard these days for people to find jobs."

"Yes... well, I did back in LA, and I also went to school... graduated from Roosevelt High."

"And what are your plans?" Lou fidgeted some more, and he could feel beads of sweat coalescing on his forehead and his underarms growing moist.

"I intend to go to college in Philly... Temple University is very affordable."

"What do you want to study?"

"English and history... I want to be a teacher... maybe also write."

"That's a fine goal, Lou. At one time, I was a teacher. I taught third and fourth grade in St. Louis Hills where I live. I may return to it one day...." Alma paused with a deep sigh and gazed out the window, leaving Lou not sure what to say and relieved when the waitress arrived with their order.

Alma and Lou ate mainly in silence, but as Lou's belly filled, he grew more composed and became curious about the fair-skinned lady seated across the table.

"What were you doing in Reno? You don't look like much of a gambler to me."

"I'm not. Not once did I enter even one of those depraved gaming establishments during my six-week sojourn!" Alma retrieved the cigarette pack, and Lou and she lit up.

"Then why were you there?"

"The same reason as thousands of women.... To get a divorce."

Lou was puzzled, and in the didactic intonation Alma had employed with her eight- and nine-year-old students, she explained to Lou that all that was

The Bus Ride

required to obtain a divorce in Reno was to stand before a judge, accompanied by an attorney, briefly explain why one wanted to end a marriage, establish residency for six weeks, and swear under oath of an intent to make Nevada one's permanent home.

"No need to fabricate a story about adultery or that my husband beat me within an inch of my life," Alma ended, deeply inhaling her cigarette and snuffing out the butt in the ashtray.

"But you're already on a bus heading back to St. Louis?" Alma blushed. "Then you did lie," Lou blurted, immediately regretting his words. Yet instead of rebuke or anger, Alma strangely smiled.

"Sometimes, Lou, a little white lie is required. You'll see as you get older, and anyway, when I made the oath, who knew? I might have decided to stay in Nevada. And surely the fifteen hundred dollars for court fees and what I had to pay the lawyer left everyone happy."

"And your husband? Did he want a divorce?" Alma's thin lips grew taut, and it was her turn to fidget.

Lou didn't know many divorced people. In fact, he couldn't think of any family or friends of his parents who officially ended their marriage either by obtaining a get from the rabbis or hiring a lawyer and going to court. Lou knew it was none of his business, but he was becoming more and more curious.

"Why did you get divorced, anyway?" Lou finally asked, breaking the silence in the wake of his previous, unanswered query.

Alma stiffened, and for an instant, Lou thought he detected a deep sadness in her eyes. Abruptly, she glanced at her watch and stood.

"C'mon, Lou, we don't have much time—just over an hour."

"An hour for what? What's to do around here before the bus leaves?"

Alma folded her arms and began tapping her foot, reminding Lou of the way every teacher he had in elementary school looked when a student misbehaved. He knew better than to dawdle. Swigging a final gulp of coffee, Lou put out his cigarette and stood.

"Where are we going?"

Alma's stern expression eased, and her body slackened in a way that Lou found surprisingly enticing.

"Just follow me. You'll see." Alma impishly smirked.

Lou trailed Alma out the door and toward a single-story, red-and-white masonry building with a sign reading Office. Alma told Lou to wait outside as she entered. A few minutes later, Alma returned swinging a key with one hand and nodded for Lou to follow. As he did, Lou noted a sprightliness to her step and a sway to her hips that he hadn't seen before. Alma led Lou to a corner building where she stopped at one of the units, unlocked and opened the door, and disappeared inside. Lou hesitated at the threshold.

"Why are we here?" Lou stammered in a state of confusion.

"Come in, Lou." Lou took a hesitant step forward and stopped. "You want to take a shower, don't you? We

The Bus Ride

probably won't get another opportunity like this for the rest of the trip. Now, hurry. We haven't much time," Alma instructed.

What Alma said made sense to Lou, and even if it didn't, he wasn't inclined to disobey. Lou looked around the room with its two beds, desk with a phone, pen and paper, and dresser on which a radio sat.

"C'mon, Lou. You go first but don't dally."

Alma slipped off her shoes and began unbuttoning her dress. Lou averted his eyes and entered the bathroom, turned on the light, closed the door, and started the shower. By the time he stripped off his clothes, the water was lukewarm just the way Lou liked it, and he stepped under the steady stream, relishing the way it sprayed on his body while he lathered up. Lou lost himself in the cascade splashing his flesh and the splattering sound on the tub, leaving him oblivious to the footsteps scampering across the bathroom floor, the swishing of the shower curtain being drawn, the feet implanting themselves firmly behind his, until suddenly he felt a body press against him while enticingly soft yet firm fingers took hold of his scrotum, rendering him helpless in their clasp.

Although Lou was conflicted and had some misgivings, he found it impossible to impede the hardening of his member or stop himself from surrendering to Alma's tugging his penis and turning him around until he was inside her as they braced themselves against the tiled wall. Lou was awash in the torrent of water. The kissing and grasping and the thrusting of their bodies left him with no idea how long he and Alma were entwined in their balancing act upon the tub's wet porcelain base. When both were spent, Alma stepped out of the tub, and all he could see through the haze was the firmness of her figure and the suppleness of her ass as she slid through the mist and disappeared into the bedroom.

Lou shut off the water, dried and dressed himself, and as much as he wanted to become invisible and transport himself into the bus and never see Alma again, he had no choice but to tread meekly into the bedroom and smile sheepishly at Alma who was in her bra and panties and slipping on knee-high stockings.

"Want one?" Alma asked, sitting on the bed with a cigarette dangling from her lips, offering the open pack to Lou, who walked over, withdrew a cigarette, and lit up, keeping the pack for himself as Alma directed.

"I'll wait for you outside," Lou said quickly turning and heading out the door before Alma could say anything further.

Stepping into the bright sunshine, Lou sneezed and shielded his eyes while securing a shaded area a few feet away. Several minutes later, Alma appeared at his side, squinting at her watch.

"We should be able to board now. I paid in advance and left the key inside so we can go directly to the bus."

That said, Alma sashayed across the parking lot with Lou a few steps behind, still in a state of confusion about what had just happened and even entertaining the possibility that it didn't occur at all but was some surreal fantasy.

Later that night, following an afternoon on the road, Alma and Lou enjoyed a fine dinner at a roadside

The Bus Ride

restaurant where Alma spoke about her life in St. Louis Hills with its tree-lined, residential streets, churches, schools and parks, and location so far west of any other heavily populated area within the municipality that it was touted as "Country Living in the City." Alma relished sharing tales with Lou about growing up in St. Louis Hills when it was still a remote, open, and forested land. How the early residents, including her family, were mostly of English stock and the names of the streets and the architecture of the houses embodied their English heritage. After college, Alma became a teacher, fell in love, and married, moving into her own home in the Hills that had been recently constructed on a lot, with a freshly seeded lawn and newly planted foliage. But her stories abruptly ended at that point, with only small talk following and Lou adroitly avoiding revealing much about himself. Their meal finished, Alma picked up the check the waitress had placed on the table.

"I don't know how to thank you, Alma, but I will repay you. Can you write down your address where I can send the money?" Alma brandished the same mischievous grin Lou had seen earlier in the day.

"No need to do that, Lou. There are some things more important than money and other ways to repay a debt." Alma rose from her seat, clasping her handbag and sauntering to the cashier with a swiveling of her hips. The sun having set, darkness enveloped the pair as they boarded the bus and took their seats on the last row, which they would exclusively occupy until reaching St. Louis.

Settled in with the window partially open and a refreshing breeze wafting against his face, Lou soon fell asleep, but for how long, he didn't know since it was still pitch black and the bus quiet except for the snoring of the nearest passenger two rows up when he was roused by fingers adroitly at work unzipping his fly and unbuttoning his trousers. Before he could speak a word, lips pressed against his where they remained implanted during the brief span of time it took for Alma to mount Lou, thrust herself onto him, and absorb his stiffening penis inside of her. Neither made a sound as the rocking intensified nor when their bodies simultaneously quivered against each other until they slackened. Saying nothing, not even giving Lou a glance, Alma rolled off and spilled into her seat. A few minutes later, her breathing eased, and deeming her asleep, Lou studied the pastel face and closed eyes. She looked so peaceful and content to Lou, and believing he had no small role to play in her serene repose, he no longer felt guilty about accepting her generosity nor bound by any financial obligation to the cryptic woman lying by his side.

Lou didn't know how long he kept still not wanting to wake Alma, but eventually, he fell into another deep sleep until he was startled by the booming voice of the bus driver who looked like the others before him and those who would follow, all wearing the same uniforms.

"Just a quick stop for gas and something to eat or wet your whistle, folks. Please return to the bus in thirty minutes." Lou glanced at Alma who turned over, facing him with her eyes fluttering.

The Bus Ride

"Want breakfast, Lou?" Alma murmured. Lou looked over at the shanty by the gas pumps and then back at Alma.

"Might be best to wait," Lou said. Alma smiled and closed her eyes.

Later that day, the bus arrived at the terminal in Denver where the driver suggested a diner across the street for lunch during the hour and a half holdover. Alma, however, had other ideas, and once on the sidewalk, she reconnoitered the surroundings, drawing her eyebrows together, fashioning a single continuous bridge above a piercing stare.

"Follow me, Lou," Alma said, turning on her heels and crossing the wide street where the six-story Hotel Shirley Savoy occupied the entire block. Lou had a notion where this was going.

"Are we having lunch there?" Lou asked.

"Are you hungry?" Alma warily eyed Lou.

"Yes. We skipped breakfast. Remember?" Alma sighed.

"All right. But let's make this quick," she said, walking past the doorman and into the lobby with Lou listlessly trailing her into the hotel's cafe. Fortunately for Lou, there was a wait for a table and service was slow, and he was even able to convince Alma to share a pie for dessert. After coffee and cigarettes, there was little time left for anything else other than returning to the bus, much to Lou's relief and Alma's chagrin.

The next major stop on the route was Kansas City, which was more than 500 miles away and wouldn't be reached until early the following morning, leaving only roadside establishments with unexceptional food options ahead. Alma spent most of the day reading the newspaper and magazines she had purchased at the depot in Denver, with Lou grudgingly accepting the publications Alma handed him each time she finished one accompanied by an admonishment that it is important to keep abreast of current events—especially with that "nasty little mustached man in Germany who's up to no good!"

It was past sunset when the bus reached the destination where the passengers could avail themselves of dinner. After pulling up to the gasoline pumps, everyone disembarked and ambled over to the white clapboard building where a flickering bulb barely illuminated the crooked sign reading Bill's Restaurant. Alma and Lou's already low expectations were not bolstered by the man presumed to be Bill, who had three-day stubble and a stained, white t-shirt and kept sticking his bald head through a gap in the wall behind the counter from which arose a concoction of noxious odors coalescing sizzling onions, blistering beef, searing fish, and anything else haphazardly tossed on the grill.

The established protocol for Bill's Restaurant was simple. After securing the customer's selections, the gaunt, gray-haired server would shuffle over to the opening in the wall and deposit the order on a shelf. Once two or three orders were scattered on the ledge, Bill's tattooed, hairy arm would reach out and snap them up. When an order was filled, Bill placed the plates on the shelf and roared, "Ready, Alice!" which invariably caused the waitress to lurch, turn, and retrieve the platters. By the time Alice hobbled over to Alma and Lou's booth, clasping pencil and

The Bus Ride

pad in her quaking hands, Lou's and Alma's appetites had abated, and they opted for a more prudent selection from the menu, requesting BLTs on toast and coffee.

Just as Lou convinced Alma to split a cherry pie for dessert, the bus driver swung open the door, shouting ten minutes till departure. Looking at Lou, Alma shrugged as she rose and sauntered to the cash register to pay. Half an hour later, with the flickering bulb above Bill's Restaurant long gone, darkness enveloped the bus while the passengers, including Lou, drifted off to sleep.

Unlike the night before, Lou was not startled when roused by the agile hand inside his trousers with its nimble fingers salaciously at play with his genitals. Nor was he surprised when Alma spilled from her seat and straddled him while guiding his penis inside her. There was the same thrashing of bodies and muffled moans of pleasure as the previous night, soon followed by abated breath, leaving Lou and Alma spent in each other's arms. What did bewilder Lou was that instead of quietly rolling back to her seat, Alma remained where she was, curling into him and then barely moving. Not knowing what to do and hoping she wasn't falling asleep, Lou kept still while listening to her breathing return to normal. But then Lou detected another sound commencing softly like a running stream and swelling into a gushing torrent crashing over rocks and swerving over boulders. Lou became alarmed when he realized that Alma was in tears, and he felt her shoulders quiver as she buried her head into his chest.

Lou thought he heard Alma murmur something, but he could not make it out. She repeated it, and Lou discerned a name—Charles. To the throb of a soothing rhythm known only to the weeping woman, Alma pitched like a buoy awash in waves of sobs, holding onto Lou as if he were an oar extended from a lifeboat. At regular intervals much like a mantra, the name Charles resonated in the dark silence. Lou patted Alma on her back, not so much to console her but to spur her to return to her seat and avoid drawing the attention of other passengers. But Alma didn't budge as she kept crying "Charles" over and over. Lou had to do something.

"Who is Charles, Alma? Is he your husband?" Lou whispered into Alma's ear while firmly gripping her quaking shoulders. Alma shook her head. "Who then?"

Alma's body stiffened, and the crying subsided. Lou could feel her gain control of herself. Alma raised her tear-stained face and replied.

"Charles is… was my son… my little boy." Lou didn't know what to say. All he could do was stare. "Charles died from rheumatic fever. He was five."

Lou knew about rheumatic fever, and there were always some kids at school getting it each year but only a few ever died.

"I… I'm sorry…" was all Lou could muster. Alma weakly raised the corners of her taut lips. "How long ago…?"

"Almost two years… that's when things went bad between John and me…. John is… or now, was… my husband." Alma answered anticipating Lou's next question. "It's not unusual for a marriage to end following the death of a child…. At least that's what I've been told…. And especially when it's the only child. John took it like

The Bus Ride

a man because, as he said, that's what men do, and he went about acting like nothing had happened. He didn't even cry at the funeral because he had to remain strong. But for whom? I didn't need strength. I needed his arms to hug me."

Alma looked at Lou with her tender emerald eyes pleading for understanding and reassurance, but Lou could only gaze back blankly, not having any idea what to say or not to say, so he said nothing. Sensing Lou's discomfiture, Alma wearily forced a smile, rolling off Lou and back to her seat. Lou lay still looking over at Alma, but she was curled up with her back to him, and he could not see if she was awake and fighting back tears or slipping into a restless slumber. Lou couldn't imagine how much it must have hurt to have her son die like that and how she must miss him. Lou thought about getting to Philadelphia and seeing his brother and his mom and... his dad....

Lou turned on his side facing Alma and reached out his arm around her shoulder. She settled back toward him, and he gently squeezed. They both remained still. Before Lou dropped off to sleep, he felt a tear roll down his cheek.

Lou slept without interruption until woken by a jolt as the bus came to a halt. The silence of the engines gave way to a cacophony of sounds. People rustling in their seats, the fumbling over outerwear, packages, and handbags, the opening of windows allowing a fresh breeze to swirl into the aisle. Lou was facing the window when he fluttered his eyes and was struck by the brightness of the sunrise. He sneezed.

"St. Louis!" The driver blared. "Right on schedule, folks. It's seven a.m."

People started filling the aisle. Lou looked over at Alma, who was already awake and returning her makeup case to her purse.

"Mister sleepyhead is finally up," Alma said with just a hint of a smile. Lou sat erect and stretched out his arms. "How about if after we retrieve our luggage, we get breakfast?" Lou was afraid Alma might not have asked, and he quickly agreed.

By the time Alma and Lou emerged from the bus, most of the passengers had vanished while those remaining huddled at the rear, awaiting their baggage. Two men, both Black, were engaged in removing the suitcases. While not outfitted like the bus drivers in Greyhound uniforms with Sam Brown belts, boots, and knickers, they were both dressed in brown trousers, open-collar shirts, tan jackets, and hats. One by one, bags were tossed by the man on the roof to the man on the ground.

"There's my suitcase," Alma said as it flew through the air to the man with outstretched arms below. Lou walked over and retrieved it. A few minutes later his bag also arrived.

Insisting on carrying both cases, Lou followed Alma to the terminal where she said the luggage could be checked while they went for breakfast. Lou saw a sign reading waiting room and walked toward the door.

"Not there, silly," Alma laughed.

"Why not? Isn't this where we leave our bags?"

The Bus Ride

"Read the sign again, Lou," Alma said with hands on her hips and a slight click of the tongue, easily easing into her schoolmarm stance.

Lou complied, and this time he noticed that just above the words waiting room, the word COLORED was written in big, bold letters. Lou turned to Alma with furrowed forehead, having no idea what it meant.

"This area is for Negroes, Lou," Alma clarified. "Ours is over there."

Alma pointed to a sign about ten feet further on, displaying the words White Waiting Room. Lou was still baffled.

"One is for the Colored and the other for us. Haven't you ever seen this before?" Alma asked heaving a sigh as she would to one of her students still unable to grasp simple addition. "Where have you been all your life?" Lou took the question literally.

"I lived mostly in Philly and for a while in Vineland, New Jersey, and these past two years in Los Angeles."

"Well, Lou, in some parts of the country, the races are kept apart as God intended. And St. Louis is one of those places. Now, let's check the baggage."

A few minutes later with claim checks in hand, Alma and Lou walked out of the terminal and into the sunshine of a pleasantly warm morning. At Alma's suggestion, Lou left his leather jacket with his suitcase, and now he was glad that he had. Being a Saturday and barely 8:00 a.m., the traffic on the thoroughfare was light. Alma glanced one way and then another, nodding for Lou to follow as she promenaded down the practically pedestrian-free sidewalk. Alma turned the corner onto a smaller street

Richard D. Bank

where Lou saw signs identifying a Chrysler, Buick, and Plymouth dealership, a Quaker State Motor Oil shop, and a Phillips 66 station. A three-story, brick building loomed across the road with the words Ozarks Coffee Shop running along the gable, which reminded Lou this meal might be his last for two days. Crossing the street with Alma, Lou couldn't figure out why a coffee shop would need such a big building until he saw more signage reading HOTEL OZARKS with rooms from $1.50 a day. Lou's heart dropped.

But as it turned out, Lou needn't have been concerned. Alma had assumed a new persona once she stepped onto the streets of St. Louis where she had lived her entire life. Not that she appeared much different to Lou, but the sultry female in the motel room at Covey's in Salt Lake City and the surreptitious seductress slinking over the backseats of the Greyhound bus in the middle of the night and the bereft woman curled into a fetal position, weeping in his arms had all receded to a place deep inside the demure lady seated across the table, ordering breakfast.

Between bites, Alma provided Lou with an overview of St. Louis so he would have a better knowledge of the city of over 800,000 inhabitants which was home to many diversified industries but had suffered more from the Depression than most metropolitan areas. Indeed, Lou was informed, thirty-five percent of the populace were without jobs; families were losing their homes; and children went to bed hungry.

Tell me about it, Lou thought to himself. He knew all about having to move and lose jobs and go days without a decent meal even before the Depression. Watching the

The Bus Ride

waitress serve their breakfast of bacon and eggs, hashed browns, toast, and coffee made Lou's mouth water, and he felt like he was the man on death row in a movie, having his last meal.

Alma informed Lou about Hooverville where 5,000 people lived in shanties stretching a mile beside the Mississippi River. How badly she feels for them and thankful to be able to reside in St. Louis Hills. Which is why she sends a check every month to one of the churches serving that community of "those poor lost souls."

"And I also give money for food baskets that The Welcome Inn distributes every day," Alma said, squaring her shoulders like a soldier about to have a medal pinned on a puffed chest.

Lou's ears perked up at this latest piece of information, and he put down the knife he had been using to spread jelly on his toast.

"The Welcome Inn.... Where is that?" Lou looked intently at Alma.

"Oh, not far from here. It's at a place called Under Free Bridge at Fourth and Chouteau, I believe...." Alma tilted her head and placed a finger to her chin. "Yes, that's where I mail my checks."

Alma and Lou finished their meal by having a smoke with their coffee and Alma handing the pack to Lou.

"I can buy another," she smiled.

The couple strolled to the bus depot where Alma claimed her luggage while Lou left his undisturbed since he had a few hours before his scheduled departure at noon. Lou carried Alma's suitcase outside. The sidewalk had become crowded with people entering and leaving the terminal, and it took a few minutes for Alma to hail a cab. Lou handed the suitcase to the driver who stored it in the trunk. Lou and Alma faced each other awkwardly shifting around and neither sure what to say. Finally, Alma extended her hand which Lou grasped.

"It's been a pleasure meeting you, Lou." Under the Greta Garbo slouch hat, Alma's green eyes twinkled, and her thin lips twisted into a coquettish smile, reminding Lou of the Alma he knew on the bus ride. "Have a safe trip."

"Thank you, Alma. Thank you for everything. And I really do want to pay you back for the meals, but I still don't know your address. I don't even know your last name!"

"No need to do that, Lou. You've paid me back already." Lou had no idea what Alma meant by that.

Alma slowly withdrew her hand from Lou's while she crouched into the taxi and closed the door. Lou remained where he stood, watching as the cabbie began to pull into traffic when Alma rolled down her window and stuck out her head.

"If it's a boy, I'm going to name him Louis," Alma grinned. The cab was swallowed into the sea of vehicles.

Chapter Seven
Vineland and the Other Alma

With the sun rapidly ascending in the clear, cerulean sky, the air was heating up, and Lou was pleased he left his leather jacket with his checked suitcase. Lou glanced at his watch and noted he had almost three hours before the bus to Philadelphia was scheduled to depart at noon, leaving him enough time, he hoped, to complete his mission. But first, Lou had to find out how to get to his destination.

Though the terminal was bustling with people, Lou thought it best to obtain directions from a local who knew the lay of the land. Spotting a cabbie stowing suitcases in the trunk of his taxi under the vigilant eyes of a well-dressed couple with stern glares and impatient faces, Lou approached the cab. A minute later, after the operation was complete, Lou asked the cabbie how he could get to The Welcome Inn at a place called Under Free Bridge.

"Just follow your nose to over there," the cabbie growled, hustling around to the driver's side of the cab and pointing to a bridge barely visible above and beyond the rooftops of the buildings nearby. "It's right under Free Bridge," he added. "Which is why they call it Under Free Bridge,"

The Bus Ride

the cabbie snickered, flashing a yellow set of crooked and broken teeth.

"Thanks," Lou said, making a beeline in the direction the cabbie had indicated, keeping his eyes fixed on the bridge that spanned the width of a vast river and loomed ever nearer as he approached.

Reaching an intersection, Lou noticed a sign reading Fourth Street, which Lou remembered Alma had mentioned, so he turned onto Fourth in the direction of the bridge. When he was within a couple of blocks of the waterway, Lou spotted a line of people snaking its way toward a building with a placard suspended from the roof emblazoned with the words The Welcome Inn. Drawing closer, Lou was unimpressed by the edifice constructed from rough planks and situated in a dingy area beneath the bridge's trestle. At the building's entrance, a handful of women wearing colorful cotton dresses hustled and bustled back and forth, retrieving small baskets and handing them to people at the front of the line. Lou found his way to the rear and took his place with about fifty supplicants ahead of him.

At first Lou was concerned he wouldn't receive a basket before having to leave and catch his bus, but the queue moved quickly. There was little talk, and the atmosphere was somber in a place where no one wanted to be but had no other choice under the circumstances—except for the volunteers, who displayed smiles and nods in response to the thank-yous and God-blesses they received in exchange for the food baskets they dispensed.

While in line, Lou took the opportunity to take in the surroundings. A few blocks in the distance and along the banks of the river, Lou saw hundreds of shacks built slipshod and in no orderly fashion, unlike anything he had ever seen before.

"What is that?" Lou asked a man wearing overalls and a cap who was standing in front of him. The man turned to Lou, staring out of vacant eyes set above splotchy cheeks.

"Hooverville," the man answered.

Lou studied the ramshackle village and recalled that Alma had spoken of it. The man turned away, leaving Lou with nothing else to do than view the people in line wearily shuffling several paces forward every minute or so. Men wearing hats or caps keeping their faces shaded from the sun and long-sleeve shirts despite the increasing warmth of the day. Some women wore small hats, but most left their heads uncovered, allowing their hair to fall toward their shoulders in tresses. Almost all the women wore plain cotton housedresses. The few children Lou noticed were either held by the hand or carried, and most of their clothing was homemade from flour and feed sacks. Lou was captivated by a woman holding a child against her chest as she patted the baby's back, and the child buried its head into her bosom. Like almost everyone else Lou observed that morning, the woman gazed listlessly somewhere toward a place far away, her eyes squinting and lips drawn, while her shoulders slouched under an invisible weight.

After half an hour, Lou reached the front of the line which had doubled in size behind him. Looking past the table covered with food baskets and through the open doors leading into the building, Lou saw coal-fired stoves built

The Bus Ride

of used brick and grates from old locomotive fireboxes. A bathtub packed with utensils floating in soapy water stood on the dirt floor. Lou was beginning to question the wisdom in seeking provisions from The Welcome Inn when he realized he was being addressed.

"Good morning," said a middle-aged woman with a cheerful face as she handed Lou a small, covered basket.

"Good morning," Lou replied uneasily accepting the food. "Thank you, ma'am."

"God bless," the woman said, picking up another basket and shifting her sight to the woman behind Lou which indicated it was time to move on.

Retracing his steps, Lou reached the bus depot with half an hour to spare before departure. After retrieving his suitcase and leather jacket, he seated himself on a bench inside the waiting room and opened the food basket, which was actually a small cardboard box with a cover. Having never been in this position before, Lou didn't know what to expect as he examined the contents: a peanut butter sandwich, a bean sandwich, spam, corn bread, two carrots, an apple, and a banana—enough food to make do for the balance of the trip. Lou had hoped for a bottle of coke or something to drink, but he still had some change in his pocket and could always get a glass of water at the stops heading home. While Lou was contemplating what he might take for an afternoon snack, he was distracted by a commotion resonating from the entranceway of the waiting area.

Closing the cover of the box, Lou looked up to see a crowd forming a semicircle near the doorway, where there appeared to be a scuffle taking place. Lou stood to get a better view but otherwise remained where he was, having no desire to get any closer. Three hatless men in shirts and trousers were in the process of dragging another man wearing a suit and a hat that somehow remained fixed to his head as he was kicking his feet along the floor. The three men doing the pulling were white while the man in tow was Black. Two of the men were grasping the arms of the Black man while the third was tugging at the struggling man's tie. Seeing the Black man gasping and his tongue extending from his open mouth, Lou thought he was witnessing some kind of horizontal lynching.

"What's happening?" Lou asked a stylishly dressed middle-aged woman who had been perched at the other end of the bench but was now standing next to Lou and rising on her toes to get a better view of the goings-on.

"Excuse me?" The woman replied knitting her eyebrows and assessing Lou with an expression that made Lou think she thought him to be an imbecile for asking such a puerile question. With a condescending sigh, the woman spoke clearly and impassively. "They're removing the nigger."

Lou winced, and the woman could see he was confused. Heaving another sigh, she elaborated further.

"This is a white-only waiting area, young man. There are signs everywhere." The woman raised her arm with a finger extended to point out several placards posted on the walls similar to the sign at the entrance Lou had seen earlier. "And even if he can't read, the nigger should know better!"

The Bus Ride

The woman harrumphed and turned away from Lou, returning her gaze upon the growing throng and the three men who now had their victim about halfway through the door being held open by several other men shouting words of encouragement.

Lou recalled the signs that Alma had pointed out designating separate waiting rooms for whites and coloreds. And indeed, the fifty or sixty people populating the waiting area, though dressed in a motley fashion, were all white folks—old and young, men and women, boys and girls—with all eyes glued upon the three men hauling the limp body out the door and hurling the contorted torso onto the concrete sidewalk.

"That'll teach this nigger a lesson and set a proper example to all niggers!" The heftiest of the trio yelled to the crowd, puffing his chest and pulling up his trousers by the belt buckle.

Lou observed some of the people murmuring their agreement and nodding their approval while others drifted away wearing blank expressions and acting as if nothing out of the ordinary had occurred. Lou turned his attention back to the woman who had been standing next to him, but she had returned to her seat at the other end of the bench. Lou was about to do the same when he heard the announcement that his bus was ready to board. He picked up his suitcase and leather jacket in one hand while holding his food basket in the other and made his way to the doorway where just a moment earlier, a man was nearly strangled to death in front of a crowd of indifferent onlookers.

Passing through the exit and onto the teeming sidewalk, the noontime sun's rays struck Lou in the eyes, and he sneezed. It was much warmer than when he had arrived at daybreak, and beads of sweat began to accumulate on his forehead. Lots of guys wore caps all year round to prevent perspiration from dripping into their eyes during the summer but not Lou, who wore a cap only in the winter to keep his head warm, though sometimes he wore a cowboy hat. There were several buses parked diagonally facing the terminal, and Lou could see his was the last one down the line. Weaving through the crowd, Lou couldn't help but notice that there were more than a few Negroes interspersed among the white people, none of whom seemed to have any objection to rubbing elbows and bumping hips with the Black populace. So why the big fuss about a Negro inadvertently entering the white waiting area to the extent that he was nearly killed? Lou just didn't understand what that was all about.

Upon reaching the front of the bus destined for Philadelphia, Lou handed his suitcase to one of two Black men wearing similar caps and shirts. Lou watched as his suitcase was tossed up to another Black man on the roof of the bus. Lou stepped up into the bus, presented his ticket to the driver, and then sauntered down the aisle, taking a seat once again at the rear row of the half-empty vehicle which was nearly full by the time it pulled away ten minutes later. Lou settled into his seat and made himself comfortable since the spot next to him remained vacant though there were passengers in the rows in front and across the aisle.

The Bus Ride

As Lou gazed out the window, the sight of the bus terminal receding in the distance was gradually replaced with the scene of the Black man with his thick tongue flapping about like a fish out of water and his torso twisting against the two sets of arms restraining him while a fleshy paw tugged at the tie around his neck rendering him barely able to breathe. Leaning back in his chair and setting his food basket on the seat next to him, Lou closed his eyes, but the image of the thrashing Black man wouldn't go away nor would Lou's perplexity about the matter. Soon, another vision replaced the scene in the St. Louis bus terminal, and it was one that had occurred almost four years earlier, on August 31, 1929, in Vineland, New Jersey, where Lou was living.

Lou wasn't sure of all the details involved in the migration of his family from Philadelphia to Vineland because it all started as a result of the failed strike his father and David Dubinsky led in 1921, when Lou was only five. Likewise, he was blissfully unaware of the catastrophic consequences of that labor strife which left Dave blacklisted and both he and Celia scrambling for work that was always "off the books" when Dave was involved. Compounding matters was the tuberculosis that began to ravage Dave's lungs, making it difficult to maintain long-term employment, which Lou was old enough to recall all too well. He could not forget, as much as he wanted to, how he'd be fighting back the tears whenever he said good-bye to his father lying limply on the couch, drained from spasms of coughing, as he and Herman would meander into the pre-dawn darkness to deliver newspapers before school.

Richard D. Bank

Yet, somehow the family managed without assistance from any of Lou's numerous aunts and uncles, often related to each other more than one way or another. Not that Dave nor Celia would have asked for a handout though deep down each knew that if they had, they likely would have been rejected since other than expressions of commiseration, nothing was ever offered. Nonetheless, they coped and always had a roof over their heads, food on the table, and clothes to wear, though for Lou that meant Herman's hand-me-downs. But barely getting by was not what Dave had wanted for his family, and a few years later, when he received an offer from his brothers Max and Sam to join them in Vineland as a partner in the Bank Brothers Clothing Factory, he leaped at the opportunity.

Other than Dave, no one in the family was happy at the prospect. At the time, Celia's three brothers and their families also resided in Strawberry Mansion, and she would miss them dearly. Indeed, Herman and Lou had grown close to many of their cousins, and both had made friends at Blaine Elementary School. But the day after completing fourth grade and the beginning of summer break, with Lou looking forward to free time in the park between his morning and late afternoon gigs selling papers on Market Street, he was informed of the pending move to Vineland.

"Next week?" Lou asked his father who was seated on a cushioned chair in the living room with a newspaper on his lap.

"Yes, Lou. It's a real opportunity and best for all of us." Dave glanced over at Celia and Herman standing a few feet away by the kitchen table.

The Bus Ride

"But I'll miss my friends... and cousins," cried Lou.

"You'll make new friends," Dave replied wearily taking a deep breath and bracing his shoulders like a fighter about to resume the next round, having just faced similar resistance from his wife and elder son. "And you'll have Max's boy, Herman, who's your age, to show you around," Dave added.

"You know, Lou," Celia said, taking a step toward him, "the train runs directly from Vineland to Philadelphia so we can visit. It's easier than getting on a bus and having to make connections. You'll see...." Celia's weepy eyes drifted off while her thin lips struggled to keep sealed a surge of words she knew was best left unsaid.

Lou glanced at Herman who was staring back with an air of resignation that Lou knew all too well. "Make the best of it," Lou could hear Herman wordlessly say. And that is what Lou did as he and the family packed their personal belongings, preparing to vacate the furnished house they rented on a month-to-month lease. By the following week, Lou's family was gone and off to Vineland.

At that time, Vineland was a borough in southern New Jersey with about 7,000 residents and stood in stark contrast to Strawberry Mansion where a larger population inhabited a much smaller space. Making for an even greater challenge to Lou and his family was that unlike the Mansion with its predominantly Jewish population, Vineland was a microcosm of the melting pot that was America.

Residing in homes constructed on spacious two-and-a-half acre plots of verdant, wooded land were

Richard D. Bank

the White Anglo-Saxon Protestants, with family trees rooted in the 1860s when the municipality was first founded as a Temperance Town, prohibiting the sale of alcohol and requiring that adequate space be provided between houses and that roads be paved to allow for the planting of flowers and shade trees. But after it was discovered that the soil was conducive to growing grapes, hence the name, Italian grape growers were enticed to establish themselves in the expanding town.

In the early decades of the twentieth century, the population almost tripled drawing workers in the poultry industry, and Vineland became known as The Egg Basket of America. Also in that era, some of the Blacks fleeing Jim Crow segregation in the South migrated to New Jersey, with more than a few finding work in Vineland—though they were unofficially restricted to reside on the "other" side of the train tracks. The one thing all groups of the population had in common was a need to clothe their bodies which was not lost on Max and Sam and resulted in the establishment of the Bank Brothers Clothing Factory in 1924, which Dave joined a year later.

Lou barely remembered anything about the building which housed the clothing factory, but he did recall Uncle Max picking up the family at the train station in a late-model Buick Touring car and driving them to have lunch at his home where he lived with his wife, Supa, and their children, Ruth and Herman. After unloading the car, Lou's family stood on a tree-lined sidewalk holding their bags and suitcases while a beaming Max

The Bus Ride

pointed to the two-story clapboard house with a white porch and both front and back yards.

"Three bedrooms," Max bellowed, "one for each of the children and the big bedroom for Supa and me. And get this—two bathrooms! Want to know the address?" Max leaned closer, simpering to his brother and sister-in-law/cousin. "It's two-eight-four-four East Oak Road. Not Thirty-first Street or Broad Street or Third Avenue but Oak Road! A real American street!"

As he stood gaping, Lou couldn't believe the structure before him housed only four people. Walking up the steps leading to the porch and the open front door where Supa stood smiling, Lou dared to dream that maybe he'd have his own bedroom in their new home.

Once inside, Max led Lou's family through each room, ending with the dining room where Herman and Ruth were seated at the table and Supa was setting the last serving dish containing deli meats. Ruth and Herman were the same ages as Lou and his brother, but they had never been close when they lived in Philadelphia and spoke little that day, though Chaim did ask Ruth about the school.

"I like it, but you'll be going to a different one," Ruth answered.

"Why? We're the same age."

"Where you'll be living is in another district... but you'll be fine, I'm sure," Ruth looked guardedly at her father.

"You'll love everything here, Dave!" Max bellowed with a broad grin. "And you'll make a ton of money at the factory. Hey! Everyone needs clothes, right?" Max laughed and all heads enthusiastically nodded.

With lunch concluded, good-byes exchanged, and promises made to get together soon, Lou's family stowed their belongings into a beat-up Model T Ford that Uncle Max said he "stole" from the dealer for a hundred bucks and that Dave could pay the business back over time. Dave slid behind the wheel and followed Max driving his Buick Touring car.

It was merely a ten-minute ride to their destination, but it seemed a world away. Uncle Max's home was situated in an area flush with foliage and trees. The houses were surrounded by lawns and demarcated by driveways and sometimes fences running along the peripheries. After a few moments trailing the Buick, the dwellings became smaller, the lots shoddier, the sidewalks barren with barely a tree in sight. A mile further on, the islands of lawns vanished, giving way to concrete, bricks, and mortar with clapboard residences interspersed amidst commercial establishments which were varied and many.

Lou's eyes widened at the panorama passing before him that included a three-story structure serving as headquarters to the Vineland Electric Company, an imposing brick building occupied by a bank, a heating company, a trucking firm, and a funeral parlor with two black hearses parked in front, leaving Lou cringing. Numerous shops dotted the landscape, with signs affixed to windows advertising their wares and services: the grocery store guaranteeing freshly picked fruits and apples, the barber promoting a two-bit haircut on Tuesdays, a kosher butcher next door to

The Bus Ride

a dilapidated, white building with a sign reading, "*Shochet* certifies kosher slaughtering," thus lending credence to the butcher's own placard promising meats and poultry were both fresh and kosher.

Lou was elated that there was not one but two bakeries, and as the car passed, he could sniff the aroma of cakes and pies floating through the open doorways. Finally, they came upon a diner with signage assuring 24-hour service that demarcated the transition from a mainly commercial zone to a predominantly residential neighborhood.

As the family drove by a stately, red-brick structure with a cement path leading to its massive, white double doors, Lou could see his mother's shoulders stiffen and his father grimace as they regarded the Baptist church with a prominent sign on its front lawn posting the hours for Sunday services. Several blocks away, there was a *shul* identifiable only by a small carving of the Ten Commandments above the doorway. No signage was needed to inform the congregants when services were held since everyone knew that three services occurred daily—at sunrise, late afternoon, and sundown—though it was often a struggle to make *minyan* that required the presence of ten men to conduct communal prayers.

Just past the *shul*, Dave followed Max when he turned onto a wider street, which Lou noted from the street sign was called Plum Street.

"I think that will be your new school, Lou," Dave shouted over his shoulder, pointing to a small, rectangular two-story building that wasn't much bigger than Uncle Max's house. "And, Chaim, the junior high is only a couple blocks away. Max says you both can walk to school, so we must be near our new home that Max arranged for us to rent."

Lou watched as the tiny building receded in the distance and thought to himself that it wasn't much bigger than the gymnasium of his elementary school in Philadelphia. Lou observed the street signs with the ordinal numbers receding from sixth to fifth to fourth to third, and then the car swerved onto the street marked Second. Dave steered toward the curb and parked right behind his brother at the corner of Second and Plum, where Lou and his family would reside for the next three years.

Uncle Max hopped out of his car and stood swinging a set of keys while watching his brother's family unload their suitcases and boxes from the old Model T.

"Follow me," Uncle Max said as he turned and walked up several steps onto the porch of the clapboard two-story building that had two front doors side by side. Over one entry the number 114 was affixed and over the other 112, where Uncle Max slid the key into the lock and opened the door. Lou would later learn that this strange structure was called a side-by-side duplex.

The front porch led into a large living room, an area with a dining table, and beyond that the kitchen which overlooked a back patio and small lawn. There was a wooden structure at the end of the driveway which Uncle Max said served as a mini warehouse for a clothing business owned by the family living at 114. After everyone had climbed the narrow staircase to the second floor, it took only a minute for Lou to realize he'd have to ditch

The Bus Ride

his dream of having his own bedroom when he saw just two bedrooms and one bathroom. To make matters worse, Lou had never seen a bedroom more minuscule than the one he'd be sharing with Herman, with a closet so shallow the boys would have to bend the clothing hangers in order to fit them in.

Though not what Lou and Herman, nor Dave and Celia, had hoped for, they were resolved to make do with their new living quarters. Handing the front door keys to his brother, Uncle Max brandished a hearty smile and departed. Lou, Herman, Dave, and Celia worked well into the night unpacking. Eventually, everyone collapsed and fell asleep, dead to the world. Lou didn't wake until the rising sun blazed through the windowpane and onto his face, triggering a sneeze when he opened his eyes. Taking advantage of being first to rise, Lou washed up in the bathroom, dressed, and went out front to see if any morning papers had been delivered.

Stepping onto the sidewalk, Lou scanned up and down the street but did not spot even one newspaper. He thought to himself that this was a good sign, and he'd try to snag a paper route first thing. Looking down at the curb, Lou noticed letters had been scribbled in white chalk. They were upside down so he walked around to read them. Knitting his eyebrows, he was puzzled by the word when his brother approached.

"What are you looking at, Lou?"

"Can't figure this out, Chaim," Lou shook his head. "The idiot who wrote this can't spell." Herman walked around and joined Lou studying the word.

"It's not misspelled, Lou."

"Yes, it is. Kick is not spelled K-I-K-E; I'm sure of that."

"The word's not kick, Lou. It sounds just the way it's spelled... kike."

"What's that?"

"It's what the *goyim* call Jews when they want to make fun of them or be mean." Lou said nothing and just looked down at the word. "It could be worse, Lou. I heard Uncle Max tell Dad that most of the *goyim* in the neighborhood are Italian and they don't pick on Jews as much as the Irish do. And there are some coloreds living not far away so maybe the wops will go after them and not bother us much."

Lou looked at his brother, only half understanding what he was talking about. Herman shrugged and turned.

"C'mon, Lou. Let's get some breakfast." Lou followed Herman into their new home at the corner of Plum and Second.

It didn't take long for the Bank family to settle into the pleasant and diverse community. Dave worked six days a week at Bank Brothers unless his health required a respite, in which case Celia added hours to her schedule at the clothing factory. Herman and Lou were busy with school and their paper routes but still had some time to make friends. On holidays and some Sundays, Dave would drive the old Model T, taking his family either to Max's house or Sam's, where everyone would gather in the backyard to partake in a lox-and-bagel spread or a buffet of cold cuts, pickles, and rye bread.

Still, Dave and Celia and the boys missed the Mansion, a neighborhood comprised primarily of Jews who for

The Bus Ride

the most part lived in multi-generational homes where the *bubbes* and *zaydes* and most of the moms and pops had emigrated from Eastern Europe and where Yiddish floated through the hallways and spilled onto the sidewalks. While Dave had his brothers in Vineland, Celia sorely missed her brother Ben, the only one of her siblings still living in Philadelphia, so whenever the opportunity arose, she'd take the train to visit, sometimes with and sometimes without Dave and the boys.

But when Celia learned late in the summer of 1928 that her brother Abe and his wife, Chaika, were returning to the old neighborhood as part of a trip back east, Celia insisted her family join her for a reunion picnic being held in Fairmount Park. Though the family had moved from Strawberry Mansion to Vineland when Lou was only nine, he could still envision Fairmount Park unfolding as far as he could see. Before him would be an endless expanse where picnickers spread their blankets and placed lawn chairs so they could read and talk and have lunch. Mostly men and a few women would volley balls over the nets on the tennis courts. Children busied themselves on the swings, seesaws, and slides. There'd be grassy knolls and spacious meadows and jagged, rocky embankments from which water trickled out of pipes and into containers held by people seeking fresh spring water to store in their refrigerators and iceboxes back home. There was nothing like it in Vineland, and Lou missed the park very much so he was excited to be there again at the family outing.

Ben, whom Celia and others affectionately called Beryl, lived with his family on Berks Street in the heart of

Strawberry Mansion. His brother Max, with whom he had operated a linen supply business known as Bank Brothers, also had resided with his family in the Mansion before his recent move to California. It wasn't clear which group of brothers, Max and Beryl or Max and Sam, first came up with the name Bank Brothers for their respective enterprises, but with one located in Pennsylvania and the other in New Jersey, it wasn't a legal concern. As for how the cousins felt about it, however, that was another matter.

"Max and Sam registered the name long before you and Max ever did," Dave chided his cousin and brother-in-law Ben as he shot a glance and a slight smile toward Celia who sighed with resignation, knowing what was likely to follow.

"We just didn't get around to the legalities until later, Dave. Who knew?" Ben shrugged.

Dave took a step closer, moving toward the center of the large picnic table covered with a checkered cloth and crammed with plates of corned beef, roast beef, salami, cheeses, pickles, jars of mustard, and a cooler packed with ice and soda bottles.

"Who knew?" Dave retorted sarcastically. "You and Max knew very well about the business in Vineland."

The two men attired in ties and jackets squared off though not one of the onlookers took them seriously since this was nothing new. Ben was five-five and Dave not much taller. Indeed, as Lou observed the feigned altercation, he assured himself that the two men couldn't do each other much harm even if they wanted to.

The Bus Ride

"*Genug!*" Dvora cried at her husband and Dave. Though able to read and write English, Dvora could not converse with comfort in a language other than Yiddish. But everyone, even the kids, understood what she meant when screaming, "Enough!" in her native tongue. Crossing her thick arms over her broad chest, her eyes glaring out of her angular face, the sturdy woman put an abrupt end to the dispute.

Relieved, Lou looked on as everyone dispersed, with his mother joining the women huddling around her niece Goldie, whose parents were Celia's brother Max and his late wife, Sura. Goldie was cuddling her baby girl under the watchful eyes of Beilah, who was hovering over the child. Lou believed Beilah was the baby's step-grandmother as well as her great aunt, having married Max after her sister Sura died when Goldie was still a child. Celia had tried explaining all this to Lou and Herman during the train ride from Vineland, adding that it was not uncommon in Russia in those times for a woman to marry a widowed brother-in-law. Nonetheless, this only compounded the confusion Lou and Herman had about who was who in the Bank clan. In any event, Lou couldn't help liking Beilah, whose broad smile seemed to be permanently etched upon her pleasant face, and he was pleased that she had joined Abe and Chaika on the trip back east though work required her husband Max to remain home.

Uncle Abe and a couple of familiar-looking men whose names Lou didn't remember smoked cigarettes and played cards while Dave and Ben strolled aimlessly on the grass, their pretended bravado a thing of the past. Lou was observing two small boys wearing short pants running around in circles while trying to figure out who was who since they were both named Albert and affectionately called Googie when he felt a tap on his shoulder.

"C'mon, Lou. It's time." Herman said with a mischievous grin.

Nothing more needed to be imparted as Lou, heart pounding, slinked off following Herman as they made their way over a verdant knoll leading to two barely visible picnic tables that were set in the center of a wooded and heavily shaded area. Not until the brothers were almost upon the tables did Lou spot the two girls, one of whom jumped up and threw her arms around Herman. She had been Herman's girlfriend before the move to Vineland. Both girls were wearing loose, dropped-waist dresses with Rose, the redhead in a blue dress, still clinging to Herman, and the other girl, clearly a couple of years younger but equally attractive, wearing a red dress. The boys felt self-conscious, having been unable to dissuade their father from requiring they wear ties and white, short-sleeve shirts, shorts, and knee-high socks, to the family reunion picnic.

"I'm Lou," Lou said, extending his hand to Rose's younger cousin.

"I'm Sarah," said the brunette, smiling shyly and taking Lou's hand.

With their fingers entwined, the two sat down on a bench while Herman and Rose drifted off. Lou had already been at boy-girl parties where couples danced to music from a radio or sometimes a record player. But the soft

The Bus Ride

touch of Sarah's skin was different, arousing Lou in a way he'd never felt before, and he couldn't seem to let go of her hand. As they both relaxed and spoke about school and the Mansion, where Sarah lived and which Lou still missed, they eased into each other until their legs and bodies rubbed together. Lou thought that this must be what Herman had been trying to explain to him about what it was like to be with a girl, when the stillness was shattered by a shrill sound coming from the top of a knoll.

"Chaim! Lou!"

It was his father's voice. Lou hastily stood withdrawing his hand from Sarah's. The bushes rustled where Herman and Rose extracted themselves appearing somewhat disheveled. Dave hollered their names repeatedly with his voice growing louder as he was approaching. With hangdog looks, Lou and Herman stumbled backward swiftly making their good-byes, and when the girls were no longer in sight, they turned and ran to their father.

"Where have you two been?" Dave cried. "It's time for the photograph. C'mon."

Hustling to catch up to their father, Herman tucked his shirttails into his shorts while Lou bristled at being deprived of the opportunity to begin a new and exciting adventure. In a few minutes, they reached the picnic area where people were placing themselves as directed by a shirt-sleeved man in a Stetson hat holding a camera whom Lou believed to be Uncle Abe. After what seemed like an eternity to Lou, who was yearning to return to the picnic tables in the woods beyond the knoll, Uncle Abe finally seemed satisfied and positioned himself about ten feet in front of the group, having secured everyone within the camera's frame. The adults stood in a row with Goldie at one end holding baby Ruth while at the other end, Ben had plunked himself with his hands in his pockets, suit jacket unbuttoned, and legs spread apart as if daring someone to get past him. In between, everyone appeared to be almost the same height: next to Goldie, Beilah stared at the camera, her arms folded below her bosom; Dave's balding head protruded like a buoy between Beilah and Celia whose arms hung stiffly at her side; Chaika was grinning at her husband holding the camera as if she was a co-conspirator with a shared secret; Sam Shineberg, the only man wearing a bow tie, looked forlorn at having been situated far from his wife, Goldie, and their daughter; and finally, Dvora stood with her hands resting on Ben's shoulder. Below on the ground, Lou's teenaged cousin Daisy kneeled, grinning at the two giggling Googies beside her; Lou sat cross-legged smiling at the camera while Herman was seated to his left, smirking about something best kept to himself. Everyone remained still and hushed as Uncle Abe snapped several shots.

"That's it, everyone!" Uncle Abe exclaimed, dropping his hand holding the camera to his side.

A sea of shoulders relaxed, sighs exhaled, feet shuffled along the lawn, and people peeled off in different directions. Lou stood watching his relatives make their farewells with kisses, handshakes, and hugs. Lou knew it wasn't likely he would be seeing Sarah anytime soon, and maybe never, and he felt let down. But then, he consoled

The Bus Ride

himself, he'd be bound to visit the Mansion again, sooner or later, so who knew….

On the train to Vineland with the sun commencing to set, Dave and Celia, Herman, and Lou, sat in their own thoughts already missing their day in the park and wishing they still lived in the Mansion. But it would be another year until they returned to make it their home once more—not because they wanted to move back, which they did, but because they had to. One reason was the Bank Brothers went out of business. The other reason was because of what transpired on August 31, 1929.

It was a warm and humid Saturday afternoon, and being a weekend, most people were off from work, making for an excellent day for a parade. The procession would take place entirely on Landis Avenue, Vineland's main thoroughfare where cars parked diagonally along the tree-lined street. The sidewalks were wide and packed with pedestrians bustling on the pavement and browsing the window displays of the stores and shops while awaiting the start of the march.

Parades were not infrequent along this route especially during the summer months, but this one had unique features that intrigued Lou and enticed him to attend along with a friend from school. Tom had been in Lou's eighth-grade class which didn't have many Jews and only one other Black kid besides Tom, which is part of what drew them together. Lou met up with Tom at the train tracks dividing where Blacks and whites lived. Tom was tall, though not as tall as Lou, but heavier with broad shoulders and sinewy arms.

Richard D. Bank

"What's so special about this parade again?" Tom asked as he joined up with Lou walking toward the center of town.

"There's going to be a broadcast."

"What's a broadcast?" Tom knitted his eyebrows.

"There will be loudspeakers along the sidewalk airing a program coming from Zarephath."

"Where's that?" Tom asked. Lou sighed as if the answer should be obvious though he only learned about all this the previous day, overhearing his dad inform Celia of the parade.

"It's about a hundred miles from here at some church called Assembly Hall where the preacher's going to be preaching. And get this, Tom…" Lou elbowed his friend while they walked along, "the preacher's a woman!"

"No way!"

"Yup. Her name's Alma White, and she's big with the KKK!" Lou said drawing himself up with an air of authority.

"The KKK! Don't you know what that is, Lou? Are you crazy taking me there?" Tom stopped dead in his tracks, forcing Lou to pause and face him.

"What are you talking about?" Lou asked shaking his head, the certainty in his voice ebbing.

"Lou, the KKK is the Klan. They wear white robes and pointed hats, and sometimes hoods cover their faces." Lou gazed dubiously at his friend. "And they like to string up Black men and boys like me and sometimes even hang them from a tree. Come to think of it, Lou, they don't care much for Jews either."

The Bus Ride

Lou's puffed chest compressed, and his shoulders slumped. He hadn't known anything about the Ku Klux Klan. All he wanted was to hear a radio broadcast booming from speakers along Landis Avenue. Explaining this to his friend, Tom came up with a compromise. They would go to the parade but watch everything from a safe distance. They wouldn't see much, and that was fine with Tom, but Lou should be able to hear what a radio broadcast outdoors sounded like. Which is exactly what the two boys did that day.

Sticking his head out from an alleyway, Lou viewed rows and rows of men strutting in the street wearing white robes and hoods, some of whom brandished flagpoles with the stars and stripes fluttering in the wind. Along the walkway, men, women, and children, accoutered in their Sunday finest though it was Saturday, waved tiny American flags, smiled, and shouted words of encouragement to the swaggering men. There was no music played, no marching band, no pretty girls twirling batons which Lou had hoped to see, so it was easy to hear the shrill, female voice blasting from the speakers obliging the marchers to stop in their tracks and the onlookers to become silent. Though he wasn't able to discern much of what was said, Lou did understand the voice of the woman preacher named Alma to be saying something about the Hebrews being everywhere, that they were a strong ally of the Roman Catholics, and that the Hebrews used their millions in gold and silver to help the Pope rule the world.

Every so often the crowd would cheer and clap their hands in response to something blaring from the speaker—especially the part about the Hebrews. When the loudspeakers fell silent, the parade resumed, and Lou and Tom scuttled out of the alley and ran off without looking back until they were far from Landis Avenue, the white-robed, marching men, and the emboldened spectators.

That evening back home after dinner, where everyone was pitching in cleaning up in the kitchen, Lou overheard his dad in a hushed voice laced with distress saying something to Celia about the parade on Landis and pogroms. Lou wasn't sure what the word pogroms meant, but he was worried that somehow his foray to the event was discovered and now he was in trouble, but his name wasn't mentioned. Lou strained to hear more, but nothing else was said about the parade or Lou's being there.

Later that night, Dave called the boys into the kitchen where Celia was seated to his side. Dave drew a deep breath and stood stiffly, making the gravity of the moment clear to the boys. Dave stated he had an announcement to make—Vineland was no longer a good place for Jews to live, and with the business gone due to the Depression, it was time to pack up and move back to Philly. At that, Celia's blue eyes glistened and though she tried to prevent her joy from being detected, she was unable to contain the grin growing across her face.

Lou was happy as well, and like his mother, it was hard to restrain himself, but he did. He was going home. Back to the Mansion, his aunts and uncles and cousins, his friends, and maybe even Sarah. Lou couldn't wait.

PART THREE

Homecoming
June 1933-May 1936

Chapter Eight
The Mansion

On Monday, June 19, 1933, at precisely 5:41 a.m., four minutes ahead of schedule, the bus carrying Lou Bank arrived at the Greyhound terminal located at Tenth and Filbert Streets in Philadelphia under the emerging shadow of William Penn's statue perched atop City Hall, the city's tallest building. Sound asleep in the last row, Lou did not wake until the bus lurched to a stop. Stretching his arms and blinking his eyes, Lou clutched his jacket and stood observing the groggy passengers ahead of him slowly filling the aisle. He stared at the box on his seat that had contained the victuals he had been given at The Welcome Inn which had sustained him the past forty-two hours and now was entirely empty. He shrugged and took his place at the end of the line listlessly filing down the aisle. Reaching the open door, Lou nodded at the bus driver and stepped down onto the parking lot just as the sun fully breached the horizon and infused the sky with its glow. Lou squinted at the rising orb and sneezed.

Resisting the impulse to take off and run until he reached his father's bedside, Lou claimed his suitcase

The Bus Ride

and sauntered to the men's room. Peering at the mirror, he barely recognized himself with his face ensconced by a reddish-brown stubble and dark shadows beneath his languid eyes. While there was nothing he could do about that, Lou did soap up and wash his hands and face. His hair disheveled and long in need of a trim, Lou opened his suitcase and withdrew the cowboy hat he sometimes wore when he was in California. What the hell, he thought, as he pulled out the cowboy boots from the suitcase to replace the scuffed shoes he'd been wearing the entire trip. Lou had no idea why he had grown to like the idea of looking like a cowboy the past year. Maybe it was because of the Western movies made in Hollywood that he would see whenever he had two bits to spare and could lose himself in a realm where good prevailed over evil, unlike the world he inhabited. In any event, he hoped that in his modified attire, no one would notice how grungy he'd become since leaving LA.

Though mid-June, it was early enough in the day for there to be a slight chill in the air, prompting Lou to slip on his leather jacket. With suitcase in hand, he walked four blocks to Broad Street, the city's main thoroughfare, where there was enough traffic for Lou to easily hitch a ride over the four miles up Broad to Ontario Street where the hospital was located. A decade had passed since Dave was first admitted to Temple University Hospital, and there had been many stays to follow. Temple turned out to be a good choice for Dave since it continued the tradition of its predecessor, the former Samaritan Hospital, to exercise indulgence when it came to timely payments from the patients, and the fact it was located not far from Strawberry Mansion made it convenient for family visits.

Two years had elapsed since Lou last walked through the massive doorway of the main entrance, but he remembered the nursing station's location where he could find out his dad's room number. Though early in the morning, people were already bustling about with the medical staff mostly in white and everyone else dressed in a motley assortment of clothing. But what everyone did seem to share was a serious demeanor, sometimes marked with concern if not outright fear. After all, Lou thought to himself, this was a hospital, and other than the doctors and nurses, why would anyone want to be here? In any event, soon he would get to see his dad, and maybe, Lou considered, things weren't as serious as his uncles had said. Perhaps Dave was even on the mend, Lou dared to hope. There had been scares before, and he bounced back. Why not now?

"Can you tell me the room number for Dave Bank?" Lou asked the only nurse at the information desk.

Without glancing up and stifling a yawn, she flipped open a ledger book and scanned several pages before settling on one. She was cute, Lou considered. Though he couldn't make out the color of her eyes, Lou could tell she was young, and her nurse's cap sat balanced atop a tuft of gleaming, blond hair. She also had a fine figure, and Lou leaned over the counter to try and catch a better glimpse. Abruptly, the nurse looked up, no longer appearing attractive. In fact, she cast an appalled scowl and seemed annoyed about something.

The Bus Ride

"Just whom are you, may I ask?"

"Lou Bank."

"A relative?"

"Yes. I'm his son."

The nurse hesitated, and then shaking her head, she said in an irritated tone of voice, "Don't you know, your father died ten days ago?"

Lou froze. His entire body—inside and out—went numb. He felt nothing. He thought nothing. His mind went blank. The tears streaming down his cheeks were not his, he was convinced. The cries Lou heard did not arise from him but came from someone else.

The nurse's glare was replaced with a sympathetic gaze, and she appeared pretty to Lou once again. Leaning forward, the nurse was about to say something, but if she did offer words of comfort, Lou did not hear them. He had already turned away from the counter with suitcase in hand and headed for the exit.

Stepping into the bright sunshine, Lou didn't sneeze. The sunlight had no effect upon his moistened eyes. He felt like throwing up, but given that his stomach was nearly empty, this seemed unlikely to Lou. His mind worked swiftly. Mom and Chaim were staying with Uncle Ben and probably would have left for work by the time he would arrive so he settled on going to Dave's sister Celia's house where Bubbe Tuba had been taking care of her son. Lou's long legs loped along Broad Street until reaching the corner where he could catch a trolley going crosstown to the depot in Strawberry Mansion, leaving him just six blocks from 31st Street where Bubbe Tuba resided with Aunt Celia, her husband, and their three children. Lou felt around in his pocket to make sure he still had a few coins to pay the fare in case he wasn't able to sneak onto the streetcar.

When Lou stepped off the trolley at the depot, he glanced across the street and beheld his beloved Fairmount Park. Much as he wanted to cross the thoroughfare, enter the park, traverse the green turf and dirt footpaths, and find some spot beneath a tree with leaf-covered branches where he could lay down and go to sleep with no obligation to ever wake up, Lou could only heave a sigh and trek down the sidewalk. By the time he reached the three-story brownstone with a covered front porch and the numerals 1946 carved on a pillar, which corresponded to the numerals Lou had scribbled on a slip of paper a week earlier along with the address of Uncle Ben's house, it was well past eight o'clock, and he figured his Uncle Joe would be at work and the kids at school. That would leave Bubbe Tuba and maybe Aunt Celia at home, which was about all the people he felt he could handle at the moment.

But Lou wasn't quite ready to make his presence known. Instead, he thought about how his *bubbe* became a young widow when his grandfather, Chaim, died back in Odessa long before Lou was born and when Dave was just a boy. Now, Lou tried to imagine the pain his *bubbe* must be feeling at losing a son though this was not her first experience with the death of a child. Though only spoken of in furtive whispers, Lou had recently pieced together that there once had been a daughter named Fannie who was raped by a Cossack. Upon learning she

The Bus Ride

was pregnant, the teenager threw herself into the Dnieper River and drowned. How Bubbe Tuba could endure outliving two children was something Lou couldn't grasp, and he wasn't sure what to say to her.

Taking a deep breath, Lou mounted the steps leading to the porch and front door where he set his suitcase on the wooden floorboards. He knocked but heard no movement inside. Perhaps Aunt Celia was out shopping or on some errand, he considered. Lou knocked again more forcefully and remembered that when they had departed for LA, Bubbe was beginning to lose some of her hearing. About to knock a third time, the door slowly opened, and his grandmother stared at him hesitantly. Lou realized how strange and bizarre he must appear with his cowboy hat and boots, bewhiskered and a suitcase by his side. Lou was no longer the nascent adolescent he was when he left Philly two years earlier.

"It's me, Bubbe. Lou."

A look of recognition slowly stretched across the round face of the wizened, gray-haired lady wearing a housedress and apron who thrust her hands upon her cheeks, shaking her head and then wrapping her ample arms around her smiling grandson. But it didn't take long before Tuba's sparkling eyes turned teary, and Lou's smile transformed to trembling lips from which spewed what sounded like the forlorn cries of a wounded fledgling.

Suddenly, Lou heard the clatter of footsteps striking the hardwood floors.

"Mama! Mama!" A woman's voice shrieked, and in an instant Aunt Celia was upon them. A short woman in her mid-thirties with dark hair, attired in a floral-print dress and thick-heeled shoes, looking as if she was preparing to head out and do some shopping, Aunt Celia ran up behind her mother, took one glimpse at the bizarrely dressed, disheveled stranger with his arms wrapped around the family matriarch, and let out a scream. Bubbe Tuba spun around and grabbed her daughter by the shoulders.

"Shush... shush, *Tziral*, it's all right." Tuba turned toward Lou. "It's Louis back from California." Celia knitted her eyebrows and craned her neck scrutinizing her nephew.

"Lou?" Celia asked appraising the tall young man, still not sure it was her deceased brother's son. Lou's cries abated, and he took a tentative step toward his aunt.

"Yes, it's me, Aunt Celia."

Hearing the voice resonating so much like Dave, Celia's stiffened shoulders eased, and she draped her arms around Lou, drawing him close to her. The threesome, comprising three generations of family, melded together sobbing and swaying as one. After a few moments, they regained their composure and seated themselves with Tuba and Celia wedged together on a small sofa and Lou buttressed in an armchair facing his aunt and grandmother, his legs crossed and arms splayed over the armrests, reminding his aunt and *bubbe* of the way Dave would seat himself exuding an air of self-assurance before TB had struck.

Over the next half hour, mother and daughter seamlessly recounted how Dave spent his final months in declining health while they tended to him. When one paused, the other immediately took up the narrative that unfolded. Everything became so real to Lou that as he gazed upon

The Bus Ride

the sofa, his aunt and *bubbe* were replaced by his father sprawled on the couch, his gaunt body contorted and ravaged by coughing spells. He envisioned Dave peering back at him—a pallid face with barren eyes that held no hope for a brighter day. Lou imagined himself reaching out to take his father's hand and squeeze it and then stand and lean over his father, kissing him above the brow just below a tiny clump of hair where there once had been a natural spit curl dipping down his forehead.

But that was not the narrative delivered by Bubbe Tuba and Aunt Celia. Instead, Lou was furnished with an exhaustive account of the last days in the life of Dave Bank and the daily visits made by his wife and elder son sometimes extending well past midnight. Finally, determined to spare Bubbe Tuba from describing the final hours of her son's life, Aunt Celia interrupted her mother and concluded the chronicle, explaining how the body was transported to be prepared and buried in accordance with Jewish law.

"On June tenth, your father died, Lou. It was a Saturday. *Shabbos.* He was buried on Monday." Lou looked at his aunt and had to restrain himself from thundering that it couldn't be—his father could not have died on June 10th. And yet, that is what the nurse also said.

"But I was told Dad was very sick with little time left and I should get here right away so I could see him before he died."

"Who told you that that?" Aunt Celia demanded to know.

"Uncle Max. He said Mom sent him a telegram."

"Which Max, Lou?" Aunt Celia leaned forward, sighing in frustration as clarification of names was something everyone in the family knew was generally required, given all the Maxes and Abes, Googies and Alberts, Chaims and Hermans, Celias, and so on.

"Oh." Lou said sheepishly. "Your Max, Aunt Celia. Your brother... Dad's brother...."

Aunt Celia's lips stiffened, and her face turned red. Lou was taken aback at the anger burning in her eyes.

"That's not what the telegram said," Celia enunciated each word as if it were sacred scripture. Seeing the perplexed look on her nephew's face, Celia continued. "I was with your mother when she sent the telegram."

Celia didn't add that she accompanied her sister-in-law, cousin, and namesake in order to pay for the cost of the telegram since Lou's mom couldn't afford even that.

"Your mother clearly told the man at Western Union that the telegram should say your dad died, that you must stay and graduate high school, and that she and Herman would be returning to LA and all of you will live there."

Lou couldn't believe what he was hearing, but it made sense. He wanted to be a teacher, and he couldn't do that without graduating high school and then attending college and that both his parents would do anything to make that happen. He also knew that more and more of the family had been migrating to California. Even now, with all of her three brothers in California, Aunt Celia was considering moving from Strawberry Mansion to LA with her family and taking Bubbe Tuba with her. But why would Uncle Max tell him....

The Bus Ride

As if reading his mind, Aunt Celia provided the answer.

"Still such a *schnorrer!*" Aunt Celia screeched, shouting to an imagined apparition of her brother hovering in midair grinning like the Cheshire cat. Turning to Tuba, she added, "Always the cheapskate, he is. OK, that's his right. But this..." Aunt Celia pointed her quaking finger at Lou, "this is unforgivable, Mom.... What he did to Lou.... This is a *shande!*"

"Not a disgrace, *Tziral*.... But not so good, either." Bubbe Tuba sighed patting her daughter on the shoulder. There was no love lost between Celia and her brother Max for reasons unknown to their mother if, indeed, there were any specific explanations at all. Tensions were to be expected within families, and though Tuba being the matriarch was generally successful keeping conflicts in check, she knew this would be difficult with the case at hand. What she did not foresee was the effect it would have on her grandson seated across from her, who was staring wide-eyed at the realization his uncles had lied to him. As he thought about it, he now understood Uncle Sam's reticence that day, and his insistence on giving Lou the leather jacket was likely motivated by a guilty conscience.

"Who do you think decided to tell me to go home? Max or Sam?" Lou asked his aunt.

"Max," Celia answered. "Your father's own brother, my brother... who else? Max is the one always taking charge. Your mother should have sent the telegram to Sam? The baby in the family?"

Lou knew Sam was the youngest of the six children born to Tuba and Chaim and the one most often doted upon. Maybe that's why he smiled so much, Lou considered. Then it all became clear to Lou who now revisited the day he was summoned to Uncle Max's house where with Uncle Sam sitting awkwardly in a corner, Max informed Lou of the impending death of his father and the need to depart without delay. Which explained why Lou's plea for a train ticket to get home sooner than by bus was denied by Uncle Max who knew there really was no rush to return given Dave was already dead. So why spend the extra money? With palms turned upward and a shrug of his shoulders, Max had beseeched Lou to understand how much of a financial burden it was for the uncles to support their nephew. Even with Lou's maternal uncles, Max and Abe, pitching in, it was not enough. What could he do, Uncle Max implored. He was only the messenger, he said.

But no. Max was not just the messenger, Lou now knew. He was in command. Aunt Celia was right. Uncle Max did a terrible thing, and Lou would never forget it. Not ever. Soon, the surging rage within him surrendered to an overwhelming wave of exhaustion—both emotional and physical. His eyelids grew heavy and his head wobbled, and Lou could no longer remain awake. Seeing this, Aunt Celia led her nephew to the stairway and up to the second floor to a bedroom shared by her boys, Abe and Hyman, who would not return from school until later in the afternoon. Lou fell upon one of the beds, and before his aunt removed his boots, he was in a sound slumber.

Lou found himself immersed in a world of dreams where his father was alive and his uncle Max was dead; where Lou lived with his parents and brother in the house

The Bus Ride

Max had once owned in Vineland but had been mystically transplanted to LA; where Dave never gasped for air nor did Lou and Herman drag themselves out of bed before dawn to hawk papers; where his mother did not have to work but could remain home and cook memorable meals for the family. Then abruptly that dreamworld shattered as Lou felt the ground vibrate from the tremors of an earthquake causing the house to come crashing down around him. There was nothing he could do. Helpless and convinced he would die, Lou felt himself being hauled by his arms to safety and away from the flailing floorboards and collapsing ceiling....

Lou bolted upright and opened his eyes. The hands shaking him by his shoulders steadied. The sun was at an angle commencing its descent when through an open window, its rays fell upon his face. Lou sneezed.

"*Gesundheit,*" his mother said with a slight laugh. "I see that my son still has his sunshine sneeze," Celia added. But the twinkle in her eyes swiftly vanished as did the grin which gave way to tears and sobs as she cuddled her youngest boy.

Pulling her head back, Celia gazed upon Lou and forced a weak smile. Lou knew it was his mother, but she seemed different. Her wide cheekbones which had always radiated strength were now covered with wrinkled, ashen skin without a single freckle in sight. There were strands of gray in her auburn hair. Celia appeared weary to Lou who surrendered himself into her embrace, hoping her hug would never end. But when Lou heard his name called and he looked up to see Herman standing by the doorway nodding at him, he withdrew from Celia's grip, sat erect, and acknowledged his brother with a bob of his head.

With little said, Lou gathered his things and made his good-byes to his *bubbe*, Aunt Celia and Uncle Joe, and their three boys, all of whom were enjoying a hearty dinner of beef brisket with thick gravy spewing an aroma reminding Lou he had had nothing to eat for almost twenty-four hours. Tempted as he was to pull up a seat and partake in the meal when invited, he joined Celia and Herman on their way out the door, onto the porch, and down to the pavement. Lou ambled alongside his mother with Herman a few steps behind while they traversed the sidewalks of Strawberry Mansion, leaving 31st Street with its three-story brownstones and reaching the narrower streets like Berks with smaller, two-story, red-brick rowhouses.

During the walk, Lou informed his mother of his last days in LA and what Uncle Max had said about the need to depart immediately and reach home before Dad died. Celia remained silent though Lou did detect a tightening of her thin lips and a grimace on her face. He knew his mother would say nothing more about the matter. His parents had been the bridge connecting two branches of the Bank family, and now the only link was Celia. She was the one always sought as someone to confide in, who would make peace when aunts and uncles or nieces and nephews or cousins argued with one another as families invariably do. And now, when she and her son were the casualties of an egregious act inflicted by one family

The Bus Ride

member upon another, she would behave no differently. Lou knew this. But Lou also knew he would not follow his mother's lead. Not this time.

Reaching their destination at 3225 Berks Street, the threesome stood at the foot of the concrete steps leading to the front door.

"It'll only be a week or so, Lou, and then we'll find a place of our own."

"But where will Lou sleep?" Herman asked. Celia looked at Herman, and after mulling over the matter for a moment, she replied wearily, "Uncle Ben will figure it out... somehow... he always does."

Uncle Ben was ten years older than Celia, and his first-born son, Sam, was already twenty-five and living on his own. The masonry rowhouse with its three large bedrooms had provided flexibility to accommodate Celia and Herman as temporary guests with Uncle Ben assigning one to them and having his son and daughter share another. As for Lou, Ben brought home a cot on which Lou could sleep in the bedroom reserved for Celia and Herman.

"A cot? You bought a cot?" Dvora questioned her husband when he carried it through the front door.

"Shush, shush, Dvora... they'll hear you," Ben glanced up the stairway where Celia and Herman were helping Lou unpack before dinner.

Dvora glared daggers and hissed, "I don't care, Beryl, if they hear me or not." Dvora twisted her head in the direction of the stairway. "They have to go. It's not right that Googie has to share a room with his sister."

"Gertie's only six, Dvora. And it's temporary."

"What did you pay for the cot, Benjamin?" Uncle Ben winced as Dvora pronounced his proper forename accompanied by the folding of her arms across her midriff.

"I paid nothing. I have it on consignment. Once they're gone, I'll sell it on installment to one of my customers. You know, dear, how quickly I can find a buyer...." Ben smiled expectantly while turning on the charm.

Dvora couldn't argue with the fact her husband had provided very well for the family, even sending Sam to pharmacy school. Presuming the matter settled, Ben called for his twelve-year-old son to help him carry the cot up the stairs.

After dinner and everyone had helped clean up, Celia and her boys retired to their bedroom exhausted and emotionally drained. Despite the fact Lou's feet extended beyond the edge of the taut, collapsible cot, he instantly fell asleep and did not even stir in the morning while Celia and Herman readied themselves for the day and the kitchen clattered with everyone hastily grabbing what they could for sustenance before going off to school or work. By the time Lou did wake, get dressed, and groggily lumber down the stairs, the only person home was Dvora adorned in a red-and-white checkered apron over her housedress, fussing about in the kitchen and clanking the utensils as she stowed them away for the next meal.

"So, Mr. Lazybones is up and about," Dvora said with a frown. Seeing the downcast expression on Lou's face and realizing a day had barely passed since he learned of his father's death, Dvora softened and added, "There's

The Bus Ride

still some jam leftover from breakfast, and I can make toast. You want coffee also?"

"Thanks, Aunt Dvora." Lou sat down at the kitchen table.

"Have you any plans for today, Lou?"

"Yes. I'm sitting *shiva*."

"What? That was last week. *Shiva* begins right after the funeral and lasts seven days, skipping Sabbath, so the last day was yesterday... though your mother and brother went back to work yesterday," she added shaking her head from side to side.

"But I wasn't here last week, Aunt Dvora. I was on a bus coming home. I didn't even know Dad died. I couldn't get to the funeral to say good-bye, and we're not allowed to visit his grave for a year—until the unveiling. So, I'm sitting *shiva* today and will stop *Shabbos* eve." Lou's jaw struck out flaunting fortitude, but his teary eyes testified otherwise.

Lou sat *shiva* in the living room. Although he was supposed to be seated on a hard stool no more than a foot or two from the ground, none was available since the *shiva* had been concluded so instead, he settled himself upon a stiff chair he retrieved from the dining room and scrutinized his surroundings. The gloomy room was filled with dark, mahogany furniture, a navy blue sofa, and brown fabric chairs. Gray-and-blue wallpaper covered the perimeter with a single window affording a view to the porch on the rare occasion its thick, purplish curtain was drawn open. A solitary lampstand set in a corner provided the only illumination except at nighttime when the area was brightened by the rays drifting in from the well-lit dining room, but by then Lou had completed his shiva-sitting for the day.

It was quiet during the time Lou sat *shiva*. Other than his aunt, no one was around, and Dvora could be gone for hours visiting friends or running errands and shopping, though more often than not, she returned with her fleshy arms empty and carrying only her handbag as she began to prepare dinner. All the family and friends had made their *shiva* calls the previous week and weren't about to pay an extra visit just for Lou. So, for almost the entire time Lou sat *shiva*, he was alone in the dismal living room of Uncle Ben's house.

Living room, Lou laughed to himself at the irony of the term when all he could think about was *death*. Lou hadn't thought much about death before. Mostly because he hadn't lost anyone close to him until then. His dad's father, Chaim, died in Russia when Dave was only seven, and Bubbe Tuba was still very much alive. Lou never knew Celia's mother, Malke, who died in Russia when Lou was four, and his maternal grandfather, Elconin, who came to America, returned before Lou was born because it wasn't religious enough. Elconin passed away a few years back though no one knew exactly when or the circumstances.

Another reason Lou hadn't given death much consideration was because of something his dad had imparted to him on the day of Lou's bar mitzvah.

"For the *goyim*, it's all about dying and going to Heaven or Hell," he recalled his father saying as he set a hand on Lou's shoulder. "Christianity is a religion focused on death. But for Jews, it's about the here and now and Life itself.

The Bus Ride

That's why the toast we made at the *kiddush* today was, 'L'chayim,' meaning, 'To Life!' As for Heaven and Hell..." his father said with a shrug, glancing at the floor and then at the ceiling above, "who knows?"

Envisioning his father's smile, Lou cried out loud and wept, stifling the sounds as best he could so no one would hear. But then, he remembered there was no one home. Lou was alone. He would never see his father again. But he would not ever forget the man who reared him and loved him, who never raised a hand and only rarely his voice to either of his sons, a man who shunned *shul* yet read the Bible every Friday following *Shabbos* dinner with his family, a man who never thought much about God one way or the other but did care about people and doing the right thing. Such were some of the thoughts Lou pondered during the three and a half days he sat *shiva* in solitude, and yet, he was not alone, accompanied as he was by the memory of his father.

Sometimes, Lou could not keep himself from nodding off, and he'd doze in the dining room chair oblivious to the world around him. He wouldn't hear Aunt Dvora return from wherever it was she had been, change into a housedress, and put on an apron before preparing dinner. He wouldn't wake up to the rattling of dishes being set on the table or the clanging of pots and pans in the kitchen. Nor would Lou be roused when Googie and Gertie charged into the house after school before joining their friends awaiting them on the sidewalk, where they'd rowdily entertain themselves. Although Lou was also impervious to the sounds of feet shuffling along the floor from those returning from work, he did respond to the gentle touch of his mother's hand on his shoulder and kiss on his cheek late that Friday afternoon marking the end of Lou's sitting *shiva*. Opening his eyes, Lou saw his mother beaming with a smile.

"I found a place for us to live, Lou. And we can move in over the weekend."

"Where, Mom?" Lou asked, sitting up and now wide awake. "Is it far? Not Vineland, I hope?" Lou wanted desperately to remain in Strawberry Mansion.

"The Plaza Apartments," Celia said. "On Thirty-third near Diamond. Across the street from the park."

"Wow... that's great! But can we afford it? I'll find work right away...."

"Don't worry, Lou. Chaim and I both have jobs... we're lucky... especially in these times...." Celia looked toward heaven and uttered, *"kine-ahora,"* to ward off the evil eye from taking away their livelihood. Lou wasn't sure of the word's derivation or exactly what *kine-ahora* meant, but he had heard it often enough to come to believe that Jews were forever fretful of tempting fate.

The next day, Celia, Lou, and Herman packed their belongings. On Sunday morning, following breakfast with Uncle Ben's family and Dvora smiling more broadly than Celia had grown accustomed to seeing and the table filled more than usual with lox, whitefish, and smoked salmon, plus a dozen bagels and mounds of cream cheese amidst the scent of sliced onions, Celia and the boys crammed Uncle Ben's car with suitcases, bags, and boxes, leaving little room for anyone other than the driver and one passenger. Waving to their uncle and mother driving off, Herman and Lou trekked down Berks until reaching a dead end across from the park. They turned onto 33rd and walked to Clifford Street, stopping at the Plaza Apartments where Uncle Ben and Celia had already began unloading the car parked in front of the twin buildings. Herman and Lou stood wide-eyed taking in the four-story structures with large, open porches and three-story columns that reminded Lou of the Victorian-style apartment houses he had seen on the occasional summer outing to Atlantic City. The location was not lost on the two brothers as they spun around and surveyed Fairmount Park and all its amenities.

"C'mon boys! You expect me and your mother to lug all this stuff up three flights of stairs?" Uncle Ben yelled.

Herman and Lou hustled over to the car and began carrying their belongings up to their third-floor apartment in the building nearest the corner. Not until the last item was unloaded did the family take the time to inspect their new living quarters. Lou immediately liked what he saw—a large area that could serve as both living and dining room, a kitchen and bathroom beyond, and finally two bedrooms, either one big enough for him and Herman to share.

"The beds and kitchen set came with the apartment," Celia said addressing her sons.

"And I'm having the rest of the furniture delivered tomorrow, Celia," said Ben. "The place will feel just like home!" Ben wrapped his arm around Celia's waist and smiled at his nephews. Leaning into his sister, he added,

"You can just give me the amount I told you on the first and third Friday of each month to pay off the balance, and in a year, you'll own the furniture free and clear!" Ben beamed broadly at his kid-sister. Herman and Lou glanced at each other, both speculating how much was in it for their uncle while watching their mother smile and kiss Ben on the cheek.

No matter, Lou thought. Suddenly he was overwhelmed by the events of the past week. Lou couldn't believe that just seven days earlier, he had stepped off the bus anxious to see his ailing father. But that didn't happen. Now, here he was in the new domicile he would share with his mother and brother. After two years in California, Lou had returned to the Mansion. He was back home. Yet, by the end of the month, he was ready to leave.

Chapter Nine
Lou Settles Down – Almost

As promised, by midday on Monday, the remaining furniture was delivered. Under the assiduous supervision of Uncle Ben, two swarthy, muscular men from whom little was heard except for frequent grunts, grimaces, and cussing, carted and lugged the bedroom bureaus, dining room table and chairs, mahogany chest of drawers, sofa, desk, and armchair for the living room, plus several lamps that struggled to provide sufficient light. Celia remained home from work and along with Lou, repositioned the furnishings as desired, filled the dressers, and set framed family photos upon every vacant surface. On one such instance, Celia broke down weeping, clutching a photograph of herself with Dave on the occasion of their marriage where she stood nestled next to her husband, leaning in with an arm over his chest while resting her hand atop his shoulder. Lou walked over and put his arm around his mother, but he couldn't find the words to say. Together they gazed at the photo until they heard Herman's approaching footsteps climbing the stairway. Celia set the picture on the dresser and walked to the kitchen, dabbing her eyes on the way.

The Bus Ride

Lou spent that week in search of work, which was a formidable task during the peak of the Great Depression. It didn't help that Lou was shy of seventeen though he generally lied, saying he was eighteen which was credible given his height and mature demeanor. But Lou soon discovered that his lack of a high school diploma and no work experience other than selling newspapers and an assortment of odd jobs in California placed him at the bottom of a long list of applicants. By Friday evening, Lou sat sullen at the dinner table, with Herman seated to his left and Celia lighting the *Shabbos* candles on the first Sabbath dinner in their new home as well as the first family *Shabbos* without Dave. Lou slept little that night, not because of his brother's occasional snoring but from mulling over all that had happened the last few weeks and what the future might hold or, perhaps more aptly, wouldn't hold.

At dawn, Lou feigned sleep while Herman dressed for work. He could hear Celia and his brother chatting as she made their breakfast. Celia had weekends off, one of the benefits for being a member of the International Ladies' Garment Workers' Union and employed at a union shop. Indeed, Celia still brimmed with pride, her cheeks turning crimson, when thinking about the wonderful words spoken at Dave's funeral by David Dubinsky, the ILGWU president and close friend of her husband. When Lou heard the door shut behind Herman, he quietly lifted himself out of bed, washed and dressed, and joined his mother having her coffee and toast in the kitchen.

"Sleep well, Lou?" Celia asked, trying to mask her concern over Lou's disappointment in not securing employment.

"Yup." Lou poured himself a cup of coffee but remained standing at the kitchen counter.

"What are your plans for today?" Lou shrugged. "Well... tomorrow comes the Sunday paper, and there will be lots of want ads. I'm sure you'll find—"

"No, I won't, Mom."

"Lou, it's been less than a week...."

"It could just as well have been a year. There's nothing around here I'm qualified to do. Not like California where I could always make a buck delivering fruit, and there was lots of outside work with no winters to interfere...."

"How about newspapers? You know you can..."

"Mom. I'm almost seventeen. Where's the future in selling newspapers? What would I have to look forward to? Being forty and owning a newspaper stand? That's the best selling papers can offer."

Celia did not reply. Her thin lips tensed, and she stiffened her back. Lou recognized Celia's defining tell that always gave her away when she ran out of answers and was compelled to acquiesce. After a moment, Celia stood and walked over to the coffee pot.

"More coffee, Lou?"

"No thanks, Mom." Lou took a final swig of coffee and set the cup on the counter. He bent down and kissed his mother on her forehead, quickly turning away so she would not see the mist glistening in his eyes.

"Where you going, Lou?"

The Bus Ride

"Just for a walk, Mom. See you later," Lou said over his shoulder, keeping his back to Celia. But he knew that was a lie. By the time he intended on returning, Celia would be at Uncle Ben's, where the family gathered every Saturday after the men returned from *shul*. And following that... Lou had other plans....

Lou stepped out the apartment door, lumbered down the flights of stairs and out onto the street. It was a warm summer morning, and the sunshine was shimmering in the cerulean sky. Lou looked up and sneezed.

Lou knew he had a long trip ahead, but he needed the walk to rid himself of the nervous energy riddling his body. A week of frustration accomplishing nothing left him weary by the end of each day and jittery at night, unable to sleep. Although he could have taken the trolley through Fairmount Park, shaving half the distance from the journey, he decided to hoof the five miles to the grocery store where Herman worked in Southwest Philadelphia near the border with Delaware County.

Lou sauntered down 33rd Street for the mile stretch opposite Fairmount Park which never left his sight. The park's benches beckoned him to cross the thoroughfare, take a seat, breathe in the fresh scents, and listen to the leaves softly thrashing in the wind that would lure him to sleep. But Lou had to move on, continuing to Girard Avenue where he turned west, crossing over the Schuylkill River. Lou paused to gaze at the rushing river a couple hundred feet beneath the bridge, and he grew dizzy and anxious. He recalled his father telling him that the span came to be called Suicide Bridge because after the market crashed and during the early years of the Depression, many despondent men leaped from the overpass seeking eternal relief below. Perhaps that explained Lou's recent acrophobia rendering him fearful of heights. Nonetheless, Lou had chosen this route and found himself frequently glancing down at the mesmerizing water.

Upon reaching 48th Street, Lou turned south toward a residential area surrounding the office and commercial buildings in Center City. In recent years, much of the neighborhood in that part of West Philadelphia had become populated with Negroes who had migrated from the Jim Crow southern states. Lou envied the Black kids enjoying themselves on a beautiful Saturday morning, reminding him of the time he was that age playing on the sidewalks of the Mansion. When Lou reached Walnut Street, he turned and walked west, traversing a commercial area that gradually gave way to a white neighborhood where he admired the imposing, three-story twin homes with covered porches that were more impressive than the rowhouses that comprised much of Strawberry Mansion.

Finally, Lou reached his destination at the intersection of 60th and Walnut Streets where a white sign affixed to a corner property proclaimed in bold red letters, Sheinberg's Grocery Store. Given the season of the year, Lou was not surprised to find numerous baskets and boxes set outside, sitting flat on the sidewalk or braced at an angle, containing apples, oranges, grapefruits, bananas, cherries, and an assortment of other fruit. Posters and placards were posted on the windows advertising some of the contents inside and their respective prices. Lou quickly surmised

The Bus Ride

that these offerings were teasers designed to entice the public to enter since Ann Page Ketchup at eight cents a bottle, ten pounds of potatoes for fifteen cents, and a loaf of white bread for six cents were real bargains.

Lou was roused from his reverie when he heard his name being called. He peered around and saw his brother emerging from the front door.

"What are you doing here?" Herman asked. His brother was dressed in a knee-length white coat with a white waistband which along with the trim mustache he recently grew, made him look older than having just turned nineteen. Rushing over to Lou, Herman gasped, "Is everything all right? Is Mom…"

"Mom's fine, Chaim. I came to talk to you." Herman sighed with relief but then knitted his slim eyebrows wondering what was up. "Got a few minutes?" Lou asked.

"Sure. Follow me." Herman spun on his heels, and Lou trailed him around the corner to the vacant stoop of a shuttered storefront, one of many businesses in the neighborhood forced to close because of the Depression.

Herman plunked himself on the top step, and Lou took the spot below while his brother extracted a pack of cigarettes from a breast pocket, withdrew two, lit them both, and handed one to Lou. The boys took a couple of drags in silence with Herman waiting patiently for his brother to say what was on his mind. Finally, Lou spoke.

"I'm leaving, Chaim. There's nothing here for me. I can't get a job, and I'll just be a burden to you and Mom."

Herman squinted at the sky in silence. He was more reticent than his younger sibling and not nearly so headstrong. He also knew Lou had likely made up his mind, and unless Herman had something new to add, there was little chance he could get Lou to think otherwise.

"Where will you go?"

"California."

"Well, I suppose that makes some sense since we have family...."

"I'm not counting on any of them, Chaim." Herman was taken aback by the harshness of Lou's tone and the glower in his eyes. He thought it wise to let the matter drop.

"Then why California?" Lou sighed and stared off in the distance while answering.

"Because LA's always warm with lots of sunshine. I can walk outside in the morning and grab a freshly squeezed glass of orange juice to drink. And there are jobs, Chaim. I can see having a future there...." Lou fixed his eyes onto Herman's. "I just don't see that here," he sighed.

"How will you get there? By bus?" There was no way Lou would do that again, and he didn't have money for a train ticket.

"I'll hitchhike."

"That's crazy, Lou," snapped Herman.

"Not so crazy," said Lou with half a smile. "The way things are these days, there's lots of folks willing to give a guy a ride. I'll have no problem."

Herman sighed, took his last draw on the cigarette, and flicked it onto the sidewalk, stamping it out with his foot. Lou did likewise.

"What did Mom say when you told her?"

The Bus Ride

"I haven't." Lou's shoulders sagged, and for the first time during the conversation, Lou lost his swagger. Herman saw his opening and took it.

"Well, my brother, that is something you are going to have to do, and there is no way you can leave before doing it." Herman stood and patted Lou on the back.

"Can you tell her for me?" Lou looked up, his azure eyes pleading, and Chaim knew his goose was cooked. He would wind up being the one to have to break his mother's heart. Unless...

"Lou, wait here. Give me five minutes. I'll be right back." Herman handed Lou another cigarette and tossed him the matches. Lou lit up and inhaled deeply watching his brother dash down the sidewalk and into the store. Before Lou could finish the cigarette, Herman was bounding back, his face beaming with a broad grin.

"Mr. Sheinberg will give you a job!" Herman blurted reaching the stoop and catching his breath.

"What?" Though Lou had heard what his brother just told him, he couldn't quite believe it was true.

"I said, you have a job, Lou. Mr. Sheinberg says you can work seventy hours a week at ten cents an hour with a Saturday or Sunday off each week."

"Really?"

"Yeah. C'mon and ask him yourself," Herman said turning and briskly walking toward the front door.

Lou followed his brother into the store where rows and rows of shelves and bins brimmed with canned goods, fresh vegetables, fruits, boxes of cereals, bottles of milk, dairy goods, bread, baked items, toiletries, cosmetic supplies, and a wide variety of other products. Women navigated the aisles clutching baskets or pushing shopping carts while intently examining the stock and scrutinizing the prices, their eyebrows warily raised. Lou estimated the space easily exceeded a thousand square feet which was larger than he had expected having viewed it from the street.

"This is my brother, Lou, Mr. Sheinberg," Lou heard Herman say, causing him to redirect his attention upon the man whom his brother was addressing.

"Hello, Lou," the man said, extending his hand which Lou grasped. Mr. Sheinberg's grip was firm, and he stared at Lou with a no-nonsense expression.

Like Herman, Mr. Sheinberg wore a white coat and waistband. He had an angular face with a pointed nose set between sable eyes. Streams of gray coursed unevenly through his jet-black hair, leaving Lou thinking that his new boss was likely past fifty. The white collar of his shirt and the Windsor knot of his tie sat under a thick, fleshy neck. Mr. Sheinberg was short and stocky, but he exuded an air of authority making it clear who was in charge.

"So, your brother told you the pay and hours?" Mr. Sheinberg crooned, sounding to Lou like the street vendors carousing the sidewalks peddling their wares and flinging Yiddishisms to potential customers, mostly ladies in floral housedresses adroit at pinching their pennies to procure the best price. Lou nodded. "*Gut.* So, when can you start?"

"Right away, sir." Lou practically shouted. Sheinberg let out a hearty laugh and smiled.

"I think we can manage without you today. You come here Monday at seven. *Vershteht?*"

The Bus Ride

"Yes."

Lou had a job. He could earn enough to contribute to the rent and food. Maybe save some and still have four bits for a date on Saturday night. Walking home, he considered something else. There was promise in the job. It was a sound establishment. He remembered Herman telling Celia how Mr. Sheinberg built the business up and could afford to send his sons to college. Maybe Mr. Sheinberg would want to sell someday, and Lou could purchase the store with what he would save from his salary. Perhaps Herman would buy it with him, and they would be partners. Of course, he and Chaim would change the store's name. It would no longer be called Sheinberg's Grocery Store. Instead, the new sign plastered over the entrance would read: Bank Brothers Groceries. Lou wouldn't have to hitchhike to California after all. Now, he had a future in Philadelphia.

That Monday morning, donning the white coat and waistband Mr. Sheinberg handed to him as the sun ascended in the sky, hurling its aura onto the streets and sidewalks surrounding Sheinberg's Grocery Store, Lou listened dutifully while the proprietor explained his newest employee's responsibilities, which commenced with unloading 100 pounds of potatoes from an idling truck. Lou looked in the direction of the vehicle when a sunbeam captured the corner of his eye, and he sneezed.

"*Gesundheit,*" said Mr. Sheinberg. "You don't have a cold, do you? We can't have you spreading germs on the fruits and vegetables," the proprietor queried, gathering his eyebrows. "If you're sick, go home, but I'll have to dock you...."

"I'm fine, Mr. Sheinberg. It's just that sometimes I sneeze in the sunshine," Lou answered brandishing a smile to make light of the situation. Mr. Sheinberg furrowed his brow and shook his head, studying Lou as if waiting to see whether a second sneeze was to follow. Finally, with a sigh and a dismissive wave of his hand, he sent Lou on his way.

"Go now," Sheinberg nodded toward the truck. "And when you're finished, sweep the floors so they're clean for our customers when we open."

Lou never incurred an idle moment working for Sheinberg. He'd have time off to eat lunch, take an occasional break with Herman and smoke a cigarette, and go to the restroom when needed and always thoroughly wash his hands afterward, which was hard to forget with a sheet of paper taped on the door instructing all employees to do so in consideration of the customers. While there was little time for much else than having dinner with his mother and brother, Lou did hang out some nights playing poker or shooting pool and on Saturday's taking a girl out for the evening.

Lou's dates were mostly unremarkable. Though seventeen, Lou could pass for twenty, being tall, mature, and a dapper dresser on date night. All he had to do was lie about his age which he effortlessly did. Thus, Lou went out with women, some not Jewish to Celia's dismay, who worked as secretaries, salesgirls, waitresses, beauticians, or in a family business, if they were fortunate enough to secure jobs in the first place. One Saturday night was much like another commencing with a movie or shagging to a

The Bus Ride

tune at a dance hall, followed by a late snack, and if Lou was lucky, something more than a kiss good night. This worked well for Lou, but by the following spring, the faces of his Saturday-night companions and the evenings spent together blended one into the other, leaving them indistinguishable and Lou beginning to think about wanting something more. Sensing this after dinner one evening, his brother summoned Lou to take a walk into the park to have a smoke.

Crossing the street and stepping onto Fairmount Park's verdant turf, the two brothers lit up and aimlessly traversed the grounds in silence. Passing the deserted tennis courts with the sun setting in the distance, Herman spoke.

"I think I'm in love, Lou."

"Rose?" Lou made it sound like a question though it really was not. Herman and Rose resumed their relationship shortly after he returned with Celia to help care for Dave, and they had been a couple ever since. Lou liked Rose. What was there not to like, he had concluded. "Any plans, Chaim?"

Herman halted, dropped his cigarette which he crushed with his heel, and faced his brother.

"We talk about it, but it's a way's off. I want Mom to be settled and..."

"I can take care of Mom, Chaim."

"I know that. But I want you to get settled too. It's less than a year since Dad died, and we all still need some time." Lou didn't reply because he knew Herman to always be cautious and patient, and there was no point in dissuading him for putting off thoughts of marriage for now. "You know, Lou, it wouldn't hurt for you to find a girl you liked a lot and go out with for more than a couple of times."

"You're not trying to marry me off, are you?" Lou laughed.

"No... nothing like that. But remember Rose's cousin Sarah?" Lou nodded. "You two seemed to hit it off."

"That was a long time ago, Chaim. We're not kids anymore."

"No, you're not. But you should see her now." Herman snickered. "She's all grown up. Graduates from high school next month."

Lou flinched at being reminded that he had been denied a high school diploma by just a couple of weeks. Herman read his brother's mind and quickly changed the subject.

"She's a doll, Lou. A nice person, and Rose and I would like to set up a double date with the two of you. What do you say?"

"Fine. Why not?" Lou shrugged, but he began to imagine what Sarah might look like and to be with her again.

The double date occurred on a mild Saturday evening at the end of April. The boys were to meet Rose and Sarah at a popular spot called Cherry's, located at 33rd and Dauphin in the heart of Strawberry Mansion, that had begun as a pushcart operated by two teenage brothers, Dave and Bernie Cherry, and later grew into a restaurant. The business became so brisk that the basement was converted to The Cherry Pit fitted with booths seating customers who could order hot dogs and fish cakes for a nickel apiece. On weeknights, the place was packed with boys and girls seeking to meet one another and sometimes

The Bus Ride

arrange impromptu parties. Everyone was dressed casually while raucous voices bounced off the plaster walls. But Saturday evenings were another matter. It was date night with the subdued patrons dressed to the nines, and snagging a table was a formidable challenge. Lou, however, knew Dave Cherry from Central High though Lou had been two years behind him, and they renewed their friendship when Lou returned from LA and began frequenting Cherry's to pick up girls.

Entering Cherry's that night, Lou smiled at Dave who was schmoozing with customers at the counter.

"All set?" Lou asked. Dave nodded with a wink.

"What's that about?" Herman asked.

"I requested a booth downstairs in the back corner."

"Why?"

"More private..."

"Why do you need privacy?" Herman asked. Lou squirmed and gazed at the floor.

"Just that I met a number of girls here, and one or two might show up tonight and..."

"Herman!" Rose's voice radiated from the direction of the front door, sparing Lou the need to explain himself further. Rose waved. She was easy to spot in the milling crowd with her crimped, red hair spilling onto her shoulders.

Approaching the girls and jostling through the mass of bodies, Lou took the opportunity to size up Sarah whom he had not seen in almost six years. He remembered the brunette hair and was not surprised to see she had grown several inches. But Lou didn't expect the fine-figured young lady with an alluring face, sloped nose, thin lips, raised eyebrows, and intense stare reminding him of Greta Garbo.

"Lou, you remember Sarah, don't you?"

Lou glanced at his brother, dismissive of the superfluous question, and offered his hand at the coyly grinning young lady before him. Sarah smoothly slid her hand into his, and its suppleness struck a chord, bringing Lou back to the summer day in the park by the picnic bench where they had first met. With reluctance, Lou released his grip so the foursome could weave their way through the congested first floor and down the stairs to The Cherry Pit and their booth in the rear corner where the brothers seated themselves across from Rose and Sarah.

The conversation flowed easily over the fish cakes and hot dogs and then the house specialty for dessert—the glacé, which was shaved ice topped with syrup served in a pointy paper cup with a cherry on top. The girls ordered cherry flavored syrup while the boys ordered orange, and by the time they finished, everyone was looking forward to more evenings together.

That spring, sometimes Lou and Sarah were joined by Rose and Herman, and other times they'd go off on their own to a movie or the park. Once, the four took the trolley to Woodside Amusement Park on a Sunday afternoon when both Lou and Herman had the day off. Lou and Sarah felt comfortable with each other, though not to the point reached by Rose and Herman who had begun talking about getting engaged. Still, they cared a great deal for one another, and after Sarah had received

The Bus Ride

her high school diploma, Lou asked about her plans as they were seated on a park bench watching people in the distance setting up lawn chairs and blankets for an impending outdoor concert at the Robin Hood Dell.

"My father wants me to go to secretarial school," Sarah answered.

"I thought you were thinking about college," said Lou. Sarah remained passive, gazing straight ahead at the setting sun. "You could easily get in, Sarah. After all, you won the mathematics award in your class!" Sarah nodded. "Then why not? It can't be the money. Your father can afford Temple's tuition, and who knows, maybe you could get a scholarship to Penn...."

"It's not that simple," said Sarah. "There are other things to consider."

"Like what?"

"Well, for one thing, my father's business is not quite what it used to be... and then there's sending my younger brothers to college...."

"It has to be more than the money that's stopping you, Sarah. If you had to, you could get part-time work. And like I said—maybe a scholarship.... What is it, really?" Sarah turned to Lou and sighed.

"What would I do with a mathematics degree?" Lou thought for a moment.

"You could teach."

"But I don't want to teach addition and subtraction to kids. I want to study more... get an advanced degree, and if I did teach—I want to teach at a college. That's just not happening, Lou."

"What do you mean?"

"How many women professors of mathematics do you know?" Lou looked blankly at Sarah before answering.

"None, I guess. But then, I don't know any college professors," laughed Lou. Sarah gave Lou a playful nudge with her elbow and feigned a stern stare.

"You know what I mean. There's no place for women in the field of mathematics...."

"Sarah, don't say that. Don't give up on your dream...."

"Why not? Didn't you?" Sarah's voice rose above her customary tranquil tone, and her eyes fixed on Lou. Shifting on the bench's wooden planks, Lou finally answered.

"It's different for me...." He weakly replied.

"How? How is it different? You want to be a teacher. You love history. But here you are, working six days a week in a grocery store, leaving little time and energy to do anything else. You talk to me about giving up on my dream? What about you giving up on yours?"

Seeing the crushed look on Lou's face, Sarah immediately regretted what she had said though Lou's silence was answer enough. She knew he had little choice but to accept the life he had. Without a high school diploma, college was out of the question, and as he had told her on their second date, his grades in California were less than satisfactory. Even if he tried, it would take a full semester to finish high school, and for now, his salary was needed for the family to make ends meet.

Sarah knew Lou was right. She had a choice though it meant standing up to her father and defiantly announcing she was going to go to college. If necessary, like Lou

The Bus Ride

had said, she could work part time and summers to pay tuition like many Temple students. She could pursue her dream. But instead, she chose to acquiesce. That was her choosing. Lou had no such option.

Sarah slid over and kissed Lou. He put his arm around her, and she rested her head on his shoulder as the sun descended, leaving the park dark except for the flickering of scattered lamplights and the faraway glow of the Robin Hood Dell where music streamed forth for the patrons' pleasure, though Lou and Sarah were too far away to hear.

That fall, Sarah did as she was told, taking courses at secretarial school in typing, stenography, and operating the adding and calculating machine, which she often found more time consuming than doing the math in her head and using pencil and paper. As New Year's Eve approached, Rose made a reservation at Gansky's Restaurant in the hub of Strawberry Mansion to celebrate not only the new year but also her cousin's employment at a Center City bank. While the foursome enjoyed their meal basked in ambience a world away from Cherry's, Lou and Sarah kept expecting Herman to withdraw a ring from his pocket and ask Rose to marry him. But that didn't occur, though it would take place the following year.

Being New Year's Eve, Lou stayed out later than usual and never heard the shrill of the alarm clock though he was aroused by his perturbed brother shaking his shoulders and barking at him to wake up. Lou groggily raised his head from the pillow.

"Sorry, Chaim. I was dead to the world."

"You better get going. You're on today," Herman grumbled returning to his bed and going back to sleep, having the day off.

Lou pulled himself upright but remained slumped on the bed, trying to recall ever having been so exhausted. Even after his morning coffee, it took all his strength to catch the trolley to reach work on time. Lou figured it was the lack of sleep that night, but as the days wore on, he still felt fatigued more often than not. One thing Lou had loved about California was that his energy did not ebb during the mild winters, and he never caught colds like he did in Philadelphia. He didn't pay much attention to his recurring coughing, but after a few weeks and Sarah's nagging, he went to see her doctor who told him he had bronchitis and it would go away. Just be patient, the patronizing physician had said. Spring would arrive soon and with it, his health would improve, Lou was assured.

But the coughing continued, and Lou kept dragging himself about, though he managed to get things done at work so Mr. Sheinberg wouldn't notice. But one early morning when Lou was unloading the weekly delivery of a hundred pounds of potatoes, his coughing became so severe that he doubled over. Sheinberg ran up to the truck with Herman on his heels just as Lou was spitting blood over his shoes.

"Are you OK?" Sheinberg asked. "What's that?" Sheinberg pointed to the red phlegm on the tips of Lou's shoes. Herman arrived and gasped, staring wide-eyed at his brother's feet. Lou nodded as he struggled to control the hacking.

The Bus Ride

"Doctor said just bronch... bronchitis.... I'll be fine," Lou spluttered. Sheinberg frowned and shook his head, having his doubts.

"Rest a while, Lou," Herman said, taking his brother by the arm. "I'll finish that. OK, Mr. Sheinberg?" Sheinberg nodded grudgingly and watched Lou limp inside the store.

Herman had a short shift that day, and by the time Lou arrived home for dinner, Celia had learned from Herman what transpired.

"I'll be fine, Mom," said Lou though his assurances did nothing to ease the creases in Celia's forehead and the fear in her eyes.

"I'm sure you will, Lou," she said, placing three bowls of simmering cabbage soup on the table. "This will help," Celia added with a forced smile. "But just to make sure, I'm calling Dr. Rubenstein in the morning so you can see him."

"Dad's doc?" Lou asked.

"Yes, the doctor who took care of dad when he had tuberculosis," Celia said. "He treats everything, Lou. Even colds and bronchitis. I'll get you an appointment." Lou swigged his soup, but what little appetite he had was gone.

Securing an appointment with Dr. Rubenstein involved nothing more than calling and making arrangements to come to the office on a specific day, which in Lou's case was his next day off. Despite protests from Lou that it was unnecessary, Celia insisted on accompanying her son to the South Philly neighborhood where Dr. Rubenstein's office was situated.

Richard D. Bank

Since the late nineteenth century, there had always been a large Jewish presence in South Philadelphia, though no one in the Bank clan had ever lived there. Russian and Polish Jews and their descendants comprised the bulk of the population east of Seventh Street while most residents west of Tenth were Italian. Dr. Rubenstein's office sat catty-corner on Ninth and Ritner Streets where the neighborhood was mixed. Though the predictable degree of prejudice and occasional animosity existed between the two ethnic groups, this did not spill over in their perceptions of physicians, and when Lou and his mother entered the waiting area of the brownstone dwelling where the medical office occupied most of the first floor, they were not surprised to hear a cacophony of Yiddish and Italian bouncing off the pale-green plaster walls. More than a dozen brown chairs backed up against three of the walls with the fourth wall barren except for the closed door leading to the doctor's office and an oil painting depicting two bloodied boxers with fists raised, stalking each other like two bulls fixing to clash.

Securing two seats in the crowded room, Lou and Celia sat in silence while every ten minutes or so, the office door would open, a patient would exit, an affable voice would call, "next," someone would stand and enter, and ten minutes or so later, the process would repeat itself. After almost an hour, with a new contingent of patients occupying the waiting area, when the doctor cried out, "next," Celia and Lou stood and crossed the threshold of the inner chamber.

Lou and Celia were seized by the scent of cigarette smoke drifting through the air. Seated at his desk, the smiling

The Bus Ride

physician was carefully extinguishing a cigarette and then tilting it in the ashtray, saving the remainder for later. Lou hadn't seen Dr. Rubenstein since they had moved to California, and the man standing and extending both hands to Celia seemed older, balder, and wearier than Lou had remembered. Lou observed the lips stiffen and eyebrows gather on the physician's face as his mother described her son's condition and fielded his series of questions.

"Take off your shirt, Lou, and have a seat," Dr. Rubenstein said, pulling out a chair by his desk. "You can sit over there, Celia," he said, indicating another chair a few feet away.

Dr. Rubenstein took Lou's blood pressure and temperature and nodded each time, but when he applied his stethoscope to Lou's chest and back, instructing Lou to take deep breaths and cough, his lips tensed and his eyebrows stretched.

"Come with me, Lou."

Lou stood and walked across the room to a door that opened into what at one time must have been a large closet but now was dark and barren except for what looked to Lou to be a huge tube about his height standing against one wall and a shiny screen situated a few feet in front of the tube.

"Just step here," Dr. Rubenstein said, pointing to the space between the two strange objects. "This is an x-ray fluoroscope, Lou, and I'm going to use it to look inside your chest at your lungs," the doctor explained. Seeing the anxious expression on Lou's face, he quickly added, "Don't worry, you won't feel a thing."

Celia looked on from where she remained seated with her hands folded and resting on the black pocketbook that sat on her lap. Her face was blank, conveying no hint of what teemed below the surface. She had been through this before. Lou hoped the doctor might smile, but he maintained his sober demeanor. Lou did as he was told, and in a few minutes, he was instructed to put his shirt back on and resume his seat by the physician's desk. Dr. Rubenstein relit his cigarette and inhaled once before snuffing it out in the half-filled ashtray. Glancing first at Lou, he turned his attention to Celia and spoke slowly.

"I'm afraid, Celia, that Lou has tuberculosis."

Chapter Ten
Bus Ride Redux

The only thing preventing Celia from flailing her arms and wailing when Dr. Rubenstein pronounced the dire prognosis was that he swiftly pitched a ray of hope for Lou and Celia to grasp the way someone thrashing in turbulent waters lunges for a tossed buoy.

"You must get Lou to Eagleville Sanatorium immediately," Dr. Rubenstein instructed Celia. "It opened eight years ago for the sole purpose of healing TB patients."

Lou and Celia leaned in trying to concentrate on what the doctor was explaining and push aside their fears of what was likely to happen if the disease could not be overcome. Dr. Rubenstein went on to explain that for an admission fee of $300, a patient was provided with a private room for ten weeks, and if a remedy was not reached in that time, the patient could remain at no charge until completely cured. It went without saying that should the patient die before the ten weeks expired, there was no pro rata refund. But this was not an issue for Celia and her son, who were crestfallen when they had to concede they just didn't have that sum of money though Lou did have almost forty dollars saved from his

The Bus Ride

salary that he had hoped to use toward buying Sheinberg's Grocery one day.

"I have thirty dollars in the coffee can," Celia added, being one of many Americans still wary of trusting their savings to financial institutions after so many bank failures in the early years of the Depression. "That's a total of seventy dollars."

"What about the family, Mom?" Lou asked. Celia frowned looking at her son's expectant gaze. Her sigh was answer enough. She turned to face Dr. Rubenstein.

"Is it possible to make weekly payments for the rest?" Celia asked hopefully, but her fretful eyes disclosed her doubt this was likely.

Dr. Rubenstein stared at Celia, then at Lou, remaining stone-faced. He had spent a decade treating her husband only to see Celia lose him in the end, and now, it was likely the same course would repeat itself with her son, who would struggle and suffer for years, only delaying the inevitable, unless he was admitted to Eagleville before it was too late. This must not happen again, Rubenstein silently vowed. Tenderly tapping Celia's hands folded on her lap, Rubenstein faintly smiled.

"Let me see what I can do," he said.

It took some time, but after contacting, cajoling, and convincing Eagleville's physicians and administrators, some of whom Dr. Rubenstein knew fairly well, Lou was scheduled to be admitted on July 3rd without having to pay more than what he and Celia had saved though there would be no private room and when healthy enough Lou would be assigned chores to perform. Dr. Rubenstein wasn't prepared for the call he received from Lou, requesting that it be delayed until July 5th since there was a vital matter he needed to attend to on the 4th, but the change was made. Lou was relieved that he hadn't been asked what could be so important since he didn't want to have to explain he intended to ask Sarah to marry him after he was well.

Before Lou was informed of his admission date to Eagleville, he and Sarah had arranged to meet at their usual bench in the park on the evening of Independence Day. Since the diagnosis, at Lou's insistence and over Sarah's strenuous objection, the time they spent together was limited to sitting at opposite ends of her front porch or on their bench in the park where they would sometimes enjoy an ice glacé from Cherry's. They also would take walks, but Lou refused to hold hands when they did.

"You can't catch TB from holding hands, Lou… or touching, either," Sarah insisted.

"I don't care what they say. We're not taking a chance…."

"Not even from a kiss, Lou! Why don't you kiss me? I miss that."

"So do I, Sarah… so do I…." Despite the fact Sarah was correct that TB was transmissible only through the air, Lou remained steadfast, and there was no more necking, which the two had grown accustomed to in the rear rows of movie theaters or on park benches after sunset or in the front seat of a car if Lou was fortunate enough to borrow one from a buddy and park off the East River Drive along the shores of the Schuylkill, amongst an assemblage of autos filled with guys and gals similarly smooching.

The Bus Ride

When they were seated facing the Robin Hood Dell where a fireworks display was scheduled at dusk, Lou asked Sarah to marry him. Inching closer to Sarah, he knew he would not be able to keep himself from kissing her once she said yes. But Sarah didn't leap off the bench and throw her arms around Lou, exclaiming, "Yes... yes... of course, yes!" Instead, Sarah fidgeted awkwardly where she sat.

"What is it, Sarah?" Lou could feel his heart race, and he fought to stifle a cough rising in his chest. Sarah couldn't bear to look at Lou as she spoke, and she averted her eyes.

"I can't marry you, Lou."

"What do you mean you can't? Don't you want to?" Sarah nodded and looked up. Lou saw the tears swell in her eyes. "Then what's stopping you?"

"My father. He says I can't marry someone with TB."

"But I'm going to get better. Dr. Rubenstein says I'm young and strong, and Eagleville has a terrific success rate. And I'm asking you to marry me only after I'm cured. We'll get officially engaged—a ring and all—the day I come home!"

"It doesn't matter. My father says TB can return. He says if we marry and have children, you could get sick again and give it to them and...."

"Your father is wrong! And what about the fact we love each other? What about that!" Sarah stared at Lou and sighed. Her tears had dissipated. Lou recognized the face of resignation. Sarah was not going to disobey her father. They would never marry, even if he no longer had TB. Maybe no one would ever marry him, even after he was well.

Without warning, rumbles roared and blasts thundered all around Lou and Sarah. They looked up to see the sky ablaze with the dazzle of bright colors coursing through the heavens. Nothing could be seen other than the flaming heavens, and nothing could be heard other than the fireworks' explosions. Sarah was oblivious to the sight of Lou's tears and the sound of his stifled coughing.

With the firework display's dwindling sparkles long gone from the night sky, the sun was struggling to break through the overcast firmament early that Friday morning. Later that evening, Celia would be covering the small dinner table with a white cloth in the center of which a silver candelabra would stand with white candles snuggly fit into each of the two candleholders. It would take all the strength she could muster to ignite the candles, solemnly sway her hands over the flickering flames, and quietly recite the blessing in the presence of two empty chairs at the table—one uninhabited for two years and destined to remain so, and another vacant for the moment, its prospects uncertain.

Lou had been awake before dawn, unable to sleep. He couldn't stop thinking about Sarah and not having a future with her while at the same time, he couldn't suppress the thought that he might not have much of a future at all. Hearing his brother quietly dressing in the dark to avoid waking him, Lou sat up in bed. Knowing Herman had to leave for work early, the two brothers had said what they had to say to each other the night before.

The Bus Ride

"I'm up, Chaim. You can put the light on. No need to trip over something and break your leg," Lou added with a fragile smile that became visible when Herman switched on the light.

The brothers somberly gazed at each other in silence. Herman walked over to Lou, bent down, and hugged him.

"I'll be back before you know it, Chaim." Herman straightened and nodded.

"I know you will. I know…" Herman couldn't say more. He turned and walked out the door and into the kitchen where Celia was brewing coffee.

Lou heard some murmurings while he dressed. He picked up his suitcase that was already packed and stepped into the hallway just as he heard the front door close. Herman was gone. He'd have to say good-bye to his mother in the absence of his brother.

Not that Celia was disposed to Lou taking the trip to Eagleville by himself. She had wanted to accompany him, but he would have none of it. The day before, Lou told his mother that he was accustomed to traveling alone, reminding her of the coast-to-coast bus journey two years earlier. But that he preferred it that way was a lie, though Lou made it sound convincing enough. The truth was Lou didn't want his mother to see him walk into a sanatorium not knowing if he would come out dead or alive.

"Morning, Mom," said Lou as he set the suitcase by the front door and sat down at the table.

"Good morning," Celia said, placing his coffee before him with milk and sugar mixed in the way he liked it. A freshly cut bagel spread with lox and cream cheese sat before him, something usually reserved for weekends along with smoked salmon, onions, tomatoes, and cucumbers. Lou wasn't hungry, but he knew he would need nourishment, and not eating would make his mother worry even more. Celia forced a smile, sitting across from Lou while sipping her coffee and watching him eat, but her eyes belied the serene façade.

Mother and son talked about everything except what was on their minds. They spoke of the weather, about Sarah and Lou splitting up, with Celia saying that things could change when Lou returned, and if not he was too young to think about marriage anyway. Which led them to both express delight that Herman and Rose would likely be married in a year or so and Celia might become a *bubbe*.

Finally, Lou finished his lox and bagel, washing down the final morsel with a gulp of coffee. Lou stood. Celia slowly rose, balancing herself with both hands trembling on the table. Lou walked over to his mother, and they looked each other in the eyes. Each one saw the same azure stare that the other saw and the same tears streaming down their cheeks.

Mother and son embraced as if it were the last time they would ever be together. They hugged and cried, squeezed and wept, until they were like wet washrags wrung out to dry. In silence, they let go of one another. Lou staggered to the door. Celia steadied herself by clutching a chair. One last glance and Lou was gone. Neither knowing if he would return.

Hoofing along 33rd Street toward Girard Avenue, Lou freed his mind from the tumultuous thoughts consuming

The Bus Ride

him ever since Dr. Rubenstein's phone call about the available bed at Eagleville. He had hoped for a sunny morning enabling Fairmount Park to bask in the beauty of its gleaming foliage, glistening leaves, and colorful flowers. Instead, the sky was filled with clouds casting a gray canopy over his beloved park, crafting a dismal haze. The park had fallen from sight when he reached the bus stop, where he set down his suitcase and waited for the #32 bus.

When Lou boarded the bus and handed the fare to the driver, it was well past the time of swelling crowds on their way to work thus leaving ample room for Lou to seat himself with his luggage by his side. Lou sat back and stared out the window, taking in the scenery of Center City, much of which was new to him, many years having passed since he last hustled up and down its sidewalks selling newspapers. He wasn't prepared for the towering buildings and waves of pedestrians flooding the teeming pavements. Nearing City Hall with its statute of William Penn perched on top, the bus veered to the right onto Market Street, where Lou got off at 16th and walked a block to Suburban Station to await the #6214 heading to Manayunk/Norristown.

Lou recalled very little of the few times he had passed through Manayunk, a hilly, residential neighborhood consisting mostly of rowhouses near the Schuylkill River in the Northwest section of the city, and he had never been to Norristown, the county seat of adjacent Montgomery County, so he was engrossed in the sights he observed as the commercial areas became fewer and the dwellings stood farther apart. Consequently, the hour-and-a-half ride passed quickly though at times Lou's head drooped, and he almost fell asleep until he recalled where he was going and why he was going there.

During the brief ride down Norristown's Main Street, Lou was surprised to see numerous stores and shops, eateries, bars, a Woolworth's, and even a theater. There were throngs of people bustling about with many hurriedly seeking a bite to eat and running errands during their lunch-hour respite. Pulling over to a zone reserved for transit vehicles, the bus screeched to a halt with the driver announcing, "End of the line!" as he swung open the door. Lou grabbed his suitcase and ambled down the aisle, stopping to ask the driver where he could pick up the bus going to Eagleville Sanatorium.

"You want the ninety-three that'll take you to the Lower Providence Township Building, and you get off there."

"Is it a long ride?"

"Nah," the driver dismissed as he warily eyed the pallid young man with the ashen face and sunken eyes lugging a damaged suitcase and inquiring about the TB hospital. The driver sidled sideways over his seat and away from Lou. "Just head over there," he snapped, pointing straight ahead, "go to the corner... there... at Markley Street." Lou looked over and saw the street sign demarcating the location.

"Thanks," Lou said, puzzled by the anxious look in the bus driver's eyes as he stepped away to disembark.

Lou ambled to the corner and waited, straddling his wobbly suitcase until the bus marked with the numerals

The Bus Ride

93 arrived. Lou informed the driver where he was headed, and after a half-hour ride through mostly countryside, the bus reached the intersection of Ridge Pike and Eagleville Road.

"You get off here," the driver shouted over his shoulder at Lou who was seated two rows behind him.

Stepping off the bus, Lou gazed at the puffs of smoke the bus belched as it disappeared down the highway, and he took in the environs. There were several scattered buildings and houses in the area, but he saw nothing remotely resembling a hospital. Beginning to fear he was in the wrong place, Lou nonetheless lifted his suitcase and turned left onto Eagleville Road as the driver had instructed. In the absence of a sidewalk, he treaded carefully on the curb and grass. The last thing he needed was to be sideswiped by some errant car, he thought.

After walking a few hundred yards, Lou reached a large sign implanted in a dirt driveway that read Eagleville Sanatorium. Perspiring profusely from the seething sun, Lou mopped the sweat from his brow as he peered down the clay road with nothing in sight. Plodding along the path for half a mile that felt much longer, Lou reached a three-story, white masonry building with a flat rooftop on which a pitched-roof structure was situated. Lou continued on the path that terminated at the pinnacle of the circular driveway which led to the building's entrance.

Lou dropped his suitcase by a towering oak double-entry door, stopping to catch his breath, and attributed his dearth of stamina to the hike, heat, and humidity. Withdrawing a cigarette from a pack in his shirt pocket,

Richard D. Bank

Lou lit up, opened one of the doors, and walked into a massive lobby with a white marble floor and a multi-colored dome three stories above, reminding Lou more of a fancy New York hotel he once saw in a movie than a hospital for people with TB. Seeking the reception desk, all Lou could see were mostly empty chairs and small tables scattered about.

"Can I help you?" Pre-occupied with taking in the surroundings, Lou hadn't noticed the young woman with a pleasant smile and bright blond hair who barely reached his shoulders appear by his side.

"I have TB, and I am here to get cured," said Lou. The girl's sparkling eyes widened and then narrowed as she scanned a clipboard with sheets of paper she had held by her side.

"Oh... you're Mr. Bank? The new patient?" Lou nodded. "Follow me, please."

Lou was barely able to keep up with the girl's brisk pace leading him across the room, down a corridor, and into an office where she offered him a seat, saying she'd be right back. Lou was still smoking his cigarette when she returned with an older woman wearing a white nurse's uniform and a scowl on her face.

"You must be crazy!" The gray-haired nurse fumed, grabbing Lou's hand holding the cigarette and pulling it away from his mouth. "You walk in here smoking with a hole in your lung? This will kill you!" The nurse yelled, pulling the cigarette out of Lou's grip and handing it like it was a piece of putrid meat to her young assistant to discard. "Get up!" She commanded.

The Bus Ride

Lou slowly stood and reached for his suitcase, but before grabbing it, he was pushed by the nurse into the hallway where she flung him onto a gurney and began to wheel him down a corridor.

"Where are you taking me? What about my suitcase?" Lou asked, gazing up at the nurse whom he noticed had a black zit at the tip of her nose.

"To your room and your things will follow. Not that you'll be needing them... at least not for a while." The nurse's anger dissipated, and she seemed slightly more kindly—but not by much. Lou fell back on the cot pondering what she meant by him not needing his things, though soon enough, he would learn for himself.

Lying on his back and staring at the pale plaster walls, Lou noted the absence of crosses that he was accustomed to seeing in many hospitals. Had he known that Eagleville Sanatorium arose from the Philadelphia Jewish Sanatorium for Consumptives that was founded three decades earlier, he would have understood that it was a secular institution. Entering a room containing two of the forty patient beds in the hospital, Lou was wheeled to the one nearest the window where the nurse deposited him, handing over hospital apparel and instructing him to stay put.

Not only did Lou stay put for the remainder of that day and night, but he stayed put for the next six weeks, never leaving the bed—not even to use the toilet. Lou did have a roommate who was twenty-two years old, had a thick head of black hair, spoke with Italian South Philly slang, and was generally congenial when not overcome by frequent coughing spells. Lou and his roommate, Tony, both shared a fondness for the younger, more supple, and attractive nurses and enjoyed playing the flirt whenever they felt up for the role.

One night during Lou's third week at Eagleville, Tony's debilitated body was intensely ravaged by the turbulence in his chest, and nighttime attendants had to wheel him out of the room. Later that morning, Lou learned that Tony had died from hemorrhaging, and he was struck by the fact that on any given night, he could be the one carted off on a gurney, never to return.

Three times a week, Lou would be taken to the operating room on the ground floor to undergo a needle aspiration performed by a doctor inserting a hollow needle with a small, flexible tube called a catheter between Lou's ribs and into the air-filled space in his lung. The doctor would then remove the needle, attach a syringe to the catheter, and withdraw the excess air. This was carefully explained to Lou the first time the procedure was performed by Dr. Harry Beloff, who was assigned to be Lou's primary physician at Eagleville.

Lou never asked, but he figured Dr. Beloff couldn't be more than ten years his senior, and there was something about him that Lou liked right away though he couldn't be sure what it was. There was little distinguishable about Dr. Beloff. He was of average height and weight, had a round face and light-brown, thinning hair, looked like a physician wearing a white shirt and dark tie with a stethoscope customarily clipped around his neck, spoke sparingly and was circumspect in his demeanor, and though he rarely laughed, he was generous with a smile.

The Bus Ride

Lou saw Dr. Beloff three times a week during the six-week needle aspiration regimen and as needed thereafter. But whenever he did see Dr. Beloff, he frequently detected a kindly sparkle in the pale-blue eyes behind the wire-framed spectacles which led Lou to conclude that was the reason he liked Dr. Beloff from the start.

After six weeks, Lou was transferred to the convalescent unit where he was permitted to get out of bed though only for meals and to use the bathroom. Every week, Lou's sputum was tested for the presence of the tuberculosis bacteria, and on the night before the first test, Lou was unable to sleep, convinced it would be positive and the aspiration treatment was a failure. But when Dr. Beloff informed him the result was negative, Lou began to hold hope he was cured, and his optimism increased with each passing week, until the following month.

"Sorry, Lou, it's positive," Dr. Beloff said in his soft-spoken tone. Lou slumped in his chair by the doctor's desk, fighting back the tears. "Not to worry, let's just see how it goes," Beloff said, setting a hand on Lou's quaking shoulder. "I think you'll be fine," he smiled.

Two weeks later, the result was negative, and it remained so for three months at which time Lou was informed by the sober-faced nurse with the black zit on her nose that he would be transferred to the Cabin.

"What's the Cabin?" Lou asked.

"It's where you'll be staying."

"For how long?"

"If all goes well, for five months."

"And then what?"

"You go home," the gray-haired nurse said with an expression that was the nearest she could muster evincing compassion.

The Cabin was situated on the sanatorium's rooftop directly behind the pitched-roof structure that Lou had seen the day he was approaching the hospital four months earlier. Taking the stairs from the third floor to the roof and assisted by an attendant carrying his suitcase, Lou made his way in the chilly November air to the small, square clapboard building and unlatched the wooden door. It was easy for Lou to see why it was called the Cabin. Except for the plaster walls, everything reminded Lou of what a cabin should look like—it was small and simple with wooden floors and two windows for ventilation. Inside, four beds were placed at one end of the area and four beds at the other end, with a hot room in the center that contained the only heater as well as a toilet, stall shower, and sink. With little outside light entering and only several scattered lightbulbs hanging from the ceiling, Lou treaded cautiously as he followed the attendant to his assigned bed. Lou questioned the attendant, who didn't appear much older than Lou, about what to expect.

"Just ask around and you'll find out," the orderly said, tossing Lou's suitcase on the bed and making a hasty retreat. By the end of the day after reconnoitering the Cabin, exploring the grounds of Eagleville, and querying his seven roommates—men ranging in age from seventeen to fifty-three, all white and gentile, all poor and dependent upon Eagleville's benevolence—Lou learned

The Bus Ride

all that he needed to know about what his life would be like in the sanatorium for however long that would be.

On the positive side, Lou ascertained that whenever he wished he could take walks anywhere on Eagleville's forty acres. On the other hand, there were chores to be performed, and for Lou that meant for the next two months, he was expected to walk the superintendent's dogs, two stubborn dachshunds named Fritz and Zigmund, twice daily. The duo generally ran Lou ragged as he tried keeping up with them on the short leash that was provided. The only time they ever appeared the least bit docile was when they returned to their master's cottage situated on the grounds. When Lou was relieved of his canine duties, his new assignment was washing and drying dishes three hours a day in the commissary.

But perhaps most important of all was what Lou learned on that first night about the five blankets folded at the foot of his bed and the crock in the shape of a pig resting on his pillow. Though still November, the Cabin was cold, and in the winter months, it would be bone chilling. Many were the times Lou would see tiny clouds of breath floating in the air. Since the sanatorium sat in an open expanse, some nights the wind whipped around the Cabin with such ferocity that the clamor made it even more difficult to sleep. Sitting on his bed shivering that evening, Lou observed his roommates perform the same procedure that he would subsequently follow.

When his turn came, Lou entered the hot room, completed the evening's ablutions, used the toilet, and lingered as long as possible to keep warm in the Cabin's only heated space. Lou then filled the pig with hot water and took it to bed with him. Nestling himself and the pig under the blankets, he cuddled the crock, savoring its warmth against his chest, and hoped he could fall asleep before the hog's heat expired. This became Lou's nightly routine until spring.

Despite his assigned tasks, taking his three daily meals in the dining hall, various medical examinations including a weekly visit with Dr. Beloff that sometimes required the needle aspiration, Lou had a good deal of time to himself. Initially, he spent most of it hanging out in the lounge, occasionally joining a poker game or playing checkers. Other times, he'd select a book from one of the half-filled shelves, preferably one by Dashiell Hammett or Agatha Christie, and find a comfortable armchair near one of the bay windows where on a sunny day, he could bask in the warm beams. Lou longed for the temperate California weather, but he had become accustomed to the cold from lurching along the grounds tugging the leash with the obstinate mongrels at the other end. Indeed, on Christmas Day, just a week after being relieved of his canine assignment and finding he missed the open air, with little for a Jew to do given the scheduled holiday activities, Lou decided to take a stroll on what was an unusually mild December afternoon.

Wearing his leather jacket and cowboy hat, Lou stepped outside under a clear blue sky and bright noonday sun and sneezed. Having no destination in mind, he ambled along aimlessly and soon found himself drifting down the dirt road, acting out the fantasy that he was healed and

The Bus Ride

could just keep on strolling until reaching the street, board a bus, and go home. Not far in the distance, he spotted a large evergreen looming in the center of a manicured lawn in front of a two-story colonial house that he had sometimes seen on his jaunts with Fritz and Zigmund. This time, however, the tree was decorated with colorful, festive ornaments, and having nowhere else to go, Lou headed there.

Advancing closer to the house, Lou spied someone on the porch rocking on a chair who seemed to be waving to him. Lou veered off the path, letting himself in through the gate and stopping several yards away from the porch.

"Hello! Merry Christmas!" A melodious, feminine voice rang out.

The woman was wearing a tailored, tan faux fur coat and a knit turban hat that Lou figured would keep her head warm. Lou smiled and cautiously approached. He couldn't determine the color of her hair stowed under the hat, but her eyes were brown, and she had a smooth-edged, pleasing face which beamed back at him. Lou stepped up on the porch and figured she was more than a few years older than he, and it was only with some effort that she was able to lift herself from the chair and extend a frail hand.

"I'm Betty," the woman said.

"I'm Lou," replied Lou, grasping her hand but not too tightly, concerned it might not withstand a firm grip.

With her coat unbuttoned, Lou discerned an agreeable figure, and wearing heels, she was almost able to look Lou directly in the eyes. But what enticed Lou even more was that during their two hours seated on the porch sharing stories about their personal lives, Betty often leaned forward—sometimes so close to Lou that he could feel the warmth of her breath on his cheeks. He found compassion in her voice as she questioned him when he spoke of his return east, his dad's death, and especially his tuberculosis, which she shared. In turn, Lou was enamored with Betty's own story.

Lou was correct that Betty was more than a few years his senior—eight, in fact. She had attended nursing school at Abington Memorial Hospital located in the northwest suburbs of the city where she secured a position following graduation. It was there that Betty was diagnosed with TB and hospitalized. Subsequently, she was dispatched to Eagleville.

"But where do you stay? Here?" Lou asked, glancing admiringly at the stonework of the house. Betty nodded.

"Yes. I rent a room on the top floor."

Lou raised his eyebrows, trying to stifle his jealousy at having to endure the Cabin's primitive accommodations. Betty stood and extended an inviting arm and open hand toward Lou.

"How about joining me inside for a hot apple cider?" Lou had never had a hot apple cider and was a little wary of entering the dwelling.

"I think I better get back... before it gets dark." Betty gazed at the sun commencing its descent in the horizon.

"Yes, you're probably right. Today is one of the shortest periods of daylight," she added. "But you will visit again, won't you?"

The Bus Ride

"Definitely," Lou said, rising from the wicker chair he had been sitting on.

Betty took a step toward the front door and removed her knit turban hat. Looking back at Lou, she smiled and tossed her head, flinging her brown hair into the air.

"How about tomorrow?" Lou asked. Betty smiled.

Amidst the rigid regimen and pervasive anxiety comprising much of Eagleville's ambience, Betty and Lou became lovers, albeit unconsummated in the sexual sense. Though they kissed and caressed in the nooks and shadows of the compound and sometimes even at night when Lou would sneak off from the Cabin and into the privacy of Betty's room, they knew that the added stress from copulation on their weakened bodies was medically prohibited. They were also circumspect about their relationship—Betty mostly because she was a very private person, and Lou mostly because he didn't feel close enough to anyone at Eagleville to confide in anyway, and he wasn't inclined to inform his mother on one of her regular Sunday visits that he was falling in love with an older, gentile woman. And if he ever even remotely considered telling her, it was certainly not on the second Sunday in January of 1936.

The snow began descending before daybreak, and by the time Lou returned to the Cabin after lunch, several inches had accumulated on the building's roof. Throwing the door open and stomping his feet, Lou spotted Henry, a man in his thirties who slept in the bunk nearest Lou.

"Hope my mom doesn't come today," Lou said to Henry.

"She can't be that crazy," Henry smirked, concealing his chagrin since no one ever visited him. In fact, the

Richard D. Bank

Cabin had few callers as most people feared infection, and those who were willing to take the risk were often discouraged from doing so by the ones they sought to call on. Though Lou protested his mother's visits, deep down he was pleased she ignored him since no one else ever came—not even Herman, who having only Sundays to spend with Rose, offered little resistance to Celia when she forbade him from undertaking the trip.

Suddenly, the Cabin's door swung open, and Celia bounded into the room accompanied by a burst of gusting snow. Lou gaped at his mother whose woolen, long coat and felt bowler hat were covered with white flakes. He stared at her rubber overshoes that had been no match for the mounting snowfall. Lou looked at the soaked face and crimson cheeks practically frozen from the cold. Seeing Lou standing by his bed, a smile swept across Celia's face, and she waived while crossing the room. Reaching her son, she wrapped her arms around him, but Lou would have none of it as he pulled apart the mitten-clad hands clasped around his neck and led his mother into the hot room where she could warm up and they could be alone.

"Mom, are you nuts? What were you thinking coming here today in this storm? You'll get pneumonia! And then what?"

Celia's lips quivered. She looked at Lou, unable to speak, her eyes awash with tears. Celia couldn't recall Lou ever having raised his voice to her before. Lou took a long, hard look at his mother, imagining how difficult it must have been to have fled Russia and trekked across Europe to reach America's shores—a wide-eyed adolescent

The Bus Ride

brimming with hope for a better life. And what came of it? Lou pondered. Two decades later, she is a widow with a son at death's doorstep, laboring long hours for barely livable wages, her life a constant struggle. And yet, he never heard her complain or speak ill of others or on Friday nights while kindling the *Shabbos* candles, ask God to ease her burden—even just a little. Lou peered into his mother's blue eyes that were gazing back at him—weary, yet still hopeful, awash with love for her younger son. Lou was mortified that he yelled at her.

Lou embraced his mother with all the might he could muster from his tuberculosis-riddled body. Celia hugged him back. They cried and held each other saying nothing except for Lou uttering something to do with begging for forgiveness and Celia responding with a nod of her head and a few Yiddish words Lou didn't understand followed by, "What is there to forgive?"

After regaining their composure, mother and son vacated the hot room and talked about the past week's events. Lou begged his mother to leave sooner than usual so she could take an earlier bus and reach home before the roads became even more treacherous. Reluctantly, Celia complied. At the Cabin's doorway, they embraced once more, and Celia retraced her footprints now barely visible in the swelling snow on her way to the stairwell, glancing over her shoulder at her son.

"See you next Sunday," she said. Lou smiled fighting back the tears.

Lou held his own during the frigid winter months, and while not getting any stronger, he did maintain what strength he had. With little sunlight to melt the Cabin's ice-laden walls and snowcapped roof, and many nights below freezing accompanied by blustery winds, Lou curled into the fetal position under his five blankets, clasping the lukewarm pig against his chest while he sought relief in sleep. More importantly, the number of needle aspirations became less frequent over the following weeks, and with it, Dr. Beloff's drawn eyebrows and furrowed forehead eased into a more tranquil terrain during their appointments. Lou began to enjoy the conversations with his physician, and they talked of things beyond the state of his health that were more personal. Lou spoke of his family, his cross-country bus trip, and his plans for going into his own business though he said nothing about Betty. In turn, Dr. Beloff informed Lou that he was looking into opening his own practice.

"In Philadelphia?" Lou asked. Dr. Beloff nodded.

"But I have to locate my office near a hospital where I'm on staff so I can admit my patients if needed and treat them. I haven't found one yet." Then Lou had an idea. The very next day, he brought the matter up with Betty.

"Don't tell anyone about this yet, but Dr. Beloff is planning on opening an office soon," Lou said to Betty as they sat on the porch taking advantage of an early spring day with tree branches beginning to bud.

"Will he remain here?" Betty asked out of concern for Lou since she had selected a different physician.

"I don't know," Lou shrugged. "I hope so or at least until after I'm well and discharged..." Lou hesitated, wishing he could take back his words since he still believed in the

The Bus Ride

Jewish superstition of giving oneself a *kine-ahora* and having the opposite of what you said come true. "Anyway, he needs to get himself on staff at a hospital first, and then he can open his office nearby. And I was thinking..." Betty looked at Lou, not having any inkling where he was going with this.

"What? What is it you're trying to say?" Betty turned facing Lou since they were sitting side by side on the loveseat that they had grown accustomed to sharing.

"Well... you worked at Abington Hospital, and it's just outside the city, and I thought you might know someone...."

"Stop right there, Lou. It's not possible." Betty sat erect, removing her hands from Lou's thighs and folding them on her lap.

"Why... why not?"

"Because he's Jewish." Lou cocked his head in surprise. Gradually, a knowing look came over Lou as though he had played this scene numerous times before in a wide range of circumstances.

"You mean they don't allow Jews in the hospital?"

"Of course, they do!" Betty laughed. "It's just the hospital does not permit physicians of the Hebrew faith to be on staff."

"They don't have any Jewish doctors?" Betty nodded. "Not even one?"

"Not even one," Betty affirmed in a tone making it clear the matter was closed.

"Well, then, I wouldn't ever want to go there even if I were dying," Lou said, squaring his shoulders and glaring at the distant trees.

With daylight growing longer and the weather balmier, Lou's stamina and health continued to improve. He and Betty would sometimes pitch a blanket in a verdant area of the grounds, and while Betty carefully set out the picnic lunch she had proficiently prepared, Lou would lay on his back, close his eyes, and sense the warmth of the sun on his face. Soon, his previously pallid skin manifested a bright, red complexion, and a spattering of dormant freckles from his childhood miraculously reappeared much to Lou's chagrin. Though not restored entirely to his former self, Lou looked and felt better than he ever had since first succumbing to tuberculosis, so it came as no surprise when Dr. Beloff informed him he was about to be discharged.

"But you still need to take it easy, Lou."

"I will, Dr. Beloff," Lou answered, though his mind was already making plans to return to work as soon as possible.

"And you may still require the needle aspiration occasionally so you'll have to make arrangements to see someone for that."

"Who should I see?"

"Well, actually, I've just opened my own practice, and I'll be happy to have you as a patient. You'll be one of my first," Dr. Beloff smiled broadly.

"Great!" Lou said. "Where is it?"

"In South Philadelphia—not far from Einstein Hospital where I'm now on staff. It's at Ninth and Ritner."

"No way, Doc. That's Dr. Rubenstein's office." Dr. Beloff was dumfounded.

"How do you know that?" Lou explained, and then Dr. Beloff added that he was sharing the space while Dr.

The Bus Ride

Rubenstein gradually retired. Lou couldn't believe his good fortune knowing he'd have not one but two of the best doctors in the city to look after him. Lou stood, and he and Dr. Beloff warmly shook hands for the last time at Eagleville.

Lou couldn't wait to tell Betty the good news. With both their conditions improving, they had been seeing more and more of each other. Lou could not understand what Betty saw in him, but he knew what he loved about her. She was smart and kind and caring which is why he figured her to be a great nurse. She always asked about him and wanted to know all about his mother and brother and if she could be of any help to Lou and his family after she was free of TB and back to her previous life. There wasn't anything Betty wouldn't do for Lou, and though he didn't say it as often as she did, he would do anything for her as well. By the time Lou received his official discharge papers, Betty and Lou believed themselves to be very much in love and were making plans to get married once Betty left Eagleville. The night before Lou's scheduled departure, while discussing where they would reside, Betty abruptly changed the subject.

"Here, Lou, I have a little something for you," Betty said, nestling closer to Lou on the loveseat and handing him a tiny box covered in floral gift-wrapping paper.

"What is this?" Lou asked, clasping the small package with both hands.

"Just a keepsake for you to remember me by," Betty said smiling. "Go on... open it." Lou quickly unwrapped the present, unfastened the tiny container, and lifted out a shiny silver dollar. "It's a newly minted 1935 silver dollar—the year we met," Betty beamed, her eyes glistening.

"But I don't have anything for you," said Lou with a downcast face.

"That's all right, hon. Just promise me you'll keep this always."

"I will.... This will never leave my side," Lou swore, placing the silver dollar in his pocket and giving his unofficial fiancée a kiss.

On a bright May morning, Lou opened the Cabin's door and stepped onto the roof with his baggage in hand. He walked to the stairwell and descended the three flights to the ground floor of the sanatorium. He smiled at everyone he saw and cried out an enthused, "Good morning!" while working his way through the corridors and out the entrance. When taking leave of Betty the night before, he promised he'd visit every Sunday until he could take her back to Philly to be with him. And after thanking Betty again for the silver dollar, Lou and Betty did more than merely make their good-byes, going beyond just kissing and caressing, both feeling well enough to consummate their love in the best possible of ways.

Lou reached the circular, concrete driveway, crossing it in the opposite direction than the one he had taken ten months earlier. When he arrived at the dirt path, he continued on his way without even a glance over his shoulder. Though he grew fatigued from the half-mile trek to the street, it was far less taxing than it had been when he had trudged over it the previous summer. Reaching the highway and the bus stop, Lou set down his suitcase. He

The Bus Ride

would have lit up a cigarette had he had one, but they were verboten at Eagleville so he could only imagine inhaling one while awaiting the bus.

    His long legs straddling the suitcase, Lou sat observing the cars and trucks passing by along with the occasional pedestrian. He looked at the trees that were filling out with green leaves. He contemplated the verdant patches bordering the walkways. He gazed at the bright blue sky, believing for the first time in a long while that he had a future after all. Then, in the distance, he saw the bus approaching. Lou stood and grasped his suitcase. Staring down the highway watching the bus grow larger as it drew near, Lou was suddenly struck by a burst of light from the rising sun on the horizon.

    Lou sneezed. And then, Lou smiled.

Author's Postscript

Dr. Harry Beloff remained Lou's doctor and close friend until his death in 1978 from cancer that was likely caused from exposure to the fluoroscope he sometimes used to examine patients in his office at Ninth and Ritner Streets.

In 1937, Herman married a woman named Rose who did have radiant red hair. They had one son whom they named David.

When Celia retired from her job in the garment industry, she was honored by the International Ladies' Garment Workers' Union. She died in 1964 much loved by her sons, grandsons, and the entire Bank clan, who still called her "Mimitziral".

After being released from Eagleville, Lou lived with Celia in a one-bedroom apartment on the top floor of a triplex. Whenever he climbed the three flights of stairs, he would get short of breath. For two months, Lou visited Betty at Eagleville until her discharge. Betty rented an apartment, and Lou moved in with her. Lou bought a fruit store with money Betty loaned him, and he worked twelve-hour days six days a week plus four hours on Sunday. Betty and Lou were married by a justice of the peace with Celia and Herman serving as witnesses. For three years, Lou and Betty were happily married, and then, in Lou's own words:

> *Betty contracted TB again and I took care of her at home. We had a single home that we rented and I made our bedroom into a kitchen and bedroom. We ate our meals together. I would cook and shop. She could have gone back to the sanitarium but she refused because she wanted to be with me. Nine months she was in bed and one night she went to the bathroom and then she called to me. I ran in and she was passed out and could hardly catch her breath. I called the police but by the time they came, she died in my arms.*

Every day, for over half a century, Lou carried a 1935 silver dollar in his pocket until one morning on a cruise ship with his family, he lost it. It was the memento Betty had given Lou to always remember her by. And he did.

In 1941, Lou began dating Ruth Frank, who at seventeen had fled Nazi Germany in 1937. After a brief time, Lou proposed to Ruth, telling her she'd have to decide right away because if they weren't to be married, he was going to drive to Los Angeles and live there. Ruth accepted Lou's proposal, and on July 5, 1941—five years to the day Lou had entered Eagleville—they were married. Lou drove that night to Atlantic City for their honeymoon, but being the July 4th holiday weekend, no rooms were available. Ruth and Lou spent their honeymoon night sleeping in the car. In the decades to follow, Lou became a highly successful real-estate developer, entrepreneur, and philanthropist.

Ruth and Lou had two sons, Richard David Bank and Kenneth Alan Bank, four grandchildren, and two great-grandchildren, one of whom is named Hayden Louis Bank.

In the summer of 1964, Lou and Ruth spent a weekend at the Concord Resort in New York's Catskill Mountains. When they returned that Sunday night, Lou asked his seventeen-year-old son Richard if he and his cousin would drive to the Concord Resort the next morning and retrieve a painting that he had seen at an auction that weekend but hadn't purchased. Lou said he already spoke with the auctioneer, and everything had been arranged.

The next day, Richard and his cousin drove three hours to Concord, picked up the oil painting after handing over a check to the auctioneer, hung around the bar eyeing girls, and then drove back home. Until writing this book, Richard never understood why this painting, now hanging in his study, was so important to his father.

The painting, by the Israeli artist Sandu Liberman, depicts a beautiful woman with a pale-blue shawl over her head, her eyes closed and her face lifted toward heaven, making the blessing over two glowing Sabbath candles set in their candelabras. Gazing at the painting one day while writing at his desk, it struck the author that the last time Lou, Herman, Celia, and Dave were all together was when they were seated at the dinner table in their Los Angeles apartment about to have what would be their final *Shabbat* dinner, and it was that memory which drew Lou to the Liberman painting. For despite all the good things that would happen in Lou's life until his death at the age of eighty-nine, there was a special place in his heart recalling his mother kindle the Sabbath candles and the glow the flickering flames cast on the faces of his family as they were about to partake in the *Shabbat* meal.

Acknowledgements

Setting is important in any novel but given that *The Bus Ride* takes place in neighborhoods and cities coast to coast, it is vital to get it right. This is no easy task given that the narrative occurs a century ago. However, in addition to the vast amount of information accessible on the internet, having lived in Philadelphia and its surrounding area my entire life, I wrote with confidence when describing most of the environs in which I placed the characters, but I did not have this benefit elsewhere in the book. Fortunately, this was alleviated by the aid of two individuals with firsthand knowledge of two other principal locales around the time of the narrative: Stan Goodman who had made Vineland his home for seven decades and Nathan Blumstein who grew up in South Philadelphia. My gratitude to each of them for having a keen eye in perceiving their surroundings and the ability to describe it to me.

Although a novel, this is a story about a very real extended family, and I felt an obligation to be as accurate as possible. This presented a myriad of challenges: insufficiency and inaccuracy of immigration/marriage/birth/death records from a hundred years ago; so many siblings, parents, aunts, uncles and cousins; two family trees coupled by a marriage of cousins; a total lack of originality in the naming of newborns leaving family members with the same names and even nicknames. As a result, I became concerned that the reader would be hopelessly lost amidst this morass of characters. To the rescue came three individuals who mitigated this predicament.

First is the principal architect of the "Bank Family Tree", Gary Bank, my second cousin who contacted me during his project. The digital version of the Bank Family Tree remained a permanent icon on my computer's desktop while writing this book. However, Gary's Tree consisted of only one branch with some reference to the second branch and I needed more. Solving this dilemma was my teenage grandson Hayden who filled in the blanks as well as taking my frequent and frantic phone calls seeking confirmation if I got the right "Max" or "Abe" or "Googie" and whether someone was both a cousin and brother-in-law to someone else. Finally, in addition to sharing conversations and reminiscences about family members from many years gone by, my brother, Ken Bank, provided me with our father's transcripts from Central High and Roosevelt High, when for the first time I learned of the egregious harm done him leading to his withdrawal from school that was a pivotal moment in his life and an essential component of this story.

While the publication process can be challenging for authors, I, on the other hand, have been fortunate to have found a tranquil and supportive haven for the publication of my last three books, including *The Bus Ride*, with Auctus Publishers, founded by Dr. Shrikrishna Singh.

As a result, I have been enabled and emboldened to be more creative and prolific than ever. Krish sets the tone for Auctus, and his passion and vision are shared by the Auctus staff.

I always envied authors when I would sometimes hear them say "my editor" with a tone of respect, appreciation, and fondness usually referring to a man with decades of experience under his belt. Now it is I who employ the same tone of voice when echoing that phrase, though "my editor", Alexa Flood, who has edited my last three books, is two generations my junior and I'm the one with all the years behind me.

When the final edited manuscript enters the production and design phase, it is placed in the competent and caring hands of Colleen Cummings, after which, I know from experience, the cover and format will emerge having captured the essence of the story when it reaches the reader. And speaking of readers, my unceasing gratitude to Ayesha Hamid, who from the day of publication is in perpetual motion making every effort to bring the book to the public's attention.

Finally, for more than half a century, I have had published well over a hundred articles, essays, book reviews, poetry, short stories and now my tenth book. Add to that scores of unpublished pieces, book proposals, and three unpublished novels and it should be clear that a substantial amount of my time and even more, my attention, has been expended often at a cost borne by others. No more so was this the case than with *The Bus Ride*, which I call my COVID book since it was written during the first two years of the pandemic when I fell into a productive pattern of spending mornings and evenings in my study escaping the present and ensconced in the past. Throughout it all, only one person has had the dubious distinction of living with me and sharing my life the past fifty-five years. To my *bashert*—Frani.

CPSIA information can be obtained
at www.ICGtesting.com
Printed in the USA
BVHW030928300323
661449BV00007B/120